Old Lady Mary

Margaret O. (Wilson) Oliphant

Contents

OLD LADY MARY

BY

Margaret O. (Wilson) Oliphant

I

She was very old, and therefore it was very hard for her to make up her mind to die. I am aware that this is not at all the general view, but that it is believed, as old age must be near death, that it prepares the soul for that inevitable event. It is not so, however, in many cases. In youth we are still so near the unseen out of which we came, that death is rather pathetic than tragic,--a thing that touches all hearts, but to which, in many cases, the young hero accommodates himself sweetly and courageously. And amid the storms and burdens of middle life there are many times when we would fain push open the door that stands ajar, and behind which there is ease for all our pains, or at least rest, if nothing more. But age, which has gone through both these phases, is apt, out of long custom and habit, to regard the matter from a different view. All things that are violent have passed out of its life,--no more strong emotions, such as rend the heart; no great labors, bringing after them the weariness which is unto death; but the calm of an existence which is enough for its needs, which affords the moderate amount of comfort and pleasure for which its being is now adapted, and of which there seems no reason that there should ever be any end. To passion, to joy, to anguish, an end must come; but mere gentle living, determined by a framework of gentle rules and habits--why should that ever be ended? When a soul has got to this retirement and is content in it, it becomes very hard to die; hard to accept the necessity of dying, and to accustom one's self to the idea, and still harder to consent to carry it out.

The woman who is the subject of the following narrative was in this position. She had lived through almost everything that is to be found in life. She had been beautiful in her youth, and had enjoyed all the triumphs of beauty; had been intoxicated with flattery, and triumphant in conquest, and mad with jealousy and the bitterness of defeat when it became evident that her day was over. She had never been a bad woman, or false, or unkind; but she had thrown herself with all her heart into those different stages of being, and had suffered as much as she enjoyed, according to the unfailing usage of life. Many a day during these storms and victories, when things went against her, when delights did not satisfy her, she had thrown out a cry into the wide air of the universe and wished to die. And then she had come to the higher table-land of life, and had borne all the spites of fortune,--had been poor and rich, and happy and sorrowful; had lost and won a hundred times over; had sat at feasts, and kneeled by deathbeds, and followed her best-beloved to the grave, often, often crying out to God above to liberate her, to make an end of her anguish, for that her strength was exhausted and she could bear no more. But she had borne it and lived through all; and now had arrived at a time when all strong sensations are over, when the soul is no longer either triumphant or miserable, and when life itself, and comfort and ease, and the warmth of the sun, and of the fireside, and the mild beauty of home were enough for her, and she required no more. That is, she required very little more, a useful routine of hours and rules, a play of reflected emotion, a pleasant exercise of faculty, making her feel herself still capable of the best things in life--of interest in her fellow-creatures, kindness to them, and a little gentle intellectual occupation, with books and men around. She had not forgotten anything in her life,--not the excitements and delights of her beauty, nor love, nor grief, nor the higher levels she had touched in her day. She did not forget the dark day when her first-born was laid in the grave, nor that triumphant and brilliant climax of her life when every one pointed to her as the mother of a hero. All these things were like pictures hung in the secret chambers of her mind, to which she could go back in silent moments, in the twilight seated by the fire, or in the balmy afternoon, when languor and sweet thoughts are over the world. Sometimes at such moments there would be heard from her a faint sob, called forth, it was quite as likely, by the recollection of the triumph as by that of the deathbed. With these pictures to go back upon at her will she was never dull, but saw herself moving through the various scenes of her life with a continual sympathy, feeling for herself in all her troubles,--sometimes approving, sometimes judging that woman who had been so pretty, so happy, so miserable, and had gone through everything that life can go through. How much that is, looking back upon it!--passages so hard that the wonder was how she could survive them; pangs so terrible that the heart would seem at its last gasp, but yet would revive and go on.

Besides these, however, she had many mild pleasures. She had a pretty house full of things which formed a graceful ***entourage*** suitable, as she felt, for such a woman as she was, and in which she took pleasure for their own beauty,--soft chairs and couches, a fireplace and lights which were the perfection of tempered warmth and illumination. She had a carriage, very comfortable and easy, in which, when the weather was suitable, she went out; and a pretty garden and lawns, in which, when she preferred staying at home, she could have her little walk, or sit out under the trees. She had books in plenty, and all the newspapers, and everything that was needful to keep her within the reflection of the busy life which she no longer cared to encounter in her own person. The post rarely brought her painful letters; for all those impassioned interests which bring pain had died out, and the sorrows of others, when they were communicated to her, gave her a luxurious sense of sympathy, yet exemption. She was sorry for them; but such catastrophes could touch her no more: and often she had pleasant letters, which afforded her something to talk and think about, and discuss as if it concerned her,--and yet did not concern her,--business which could not hurt her if it failed, which would please her if it succeeded. Her letters, her papers, her books, each coming at its appointed hour, were all instruments of pleasure. She came down-stairs at a certain hour, which she kept to as if it had been of the utmost importance, although it was of no importance at all: she took just so much good wine, so many cups of tea. Her repasts were as regular as clockwork--never too late, never too early. Her whole life went on velvet, rolling smoothly along, without jar or interruption, blameless, pleasant, kind. People talked of her old age as a model of old age, with no bitterness or sourness in it. And, indeed, why should she have been sour or bitter? It suited her far better to be kind. She was in reality kind to everybody, liking to see pleasant faces about her. The poor had no reason to complain of her; her servants were very comfortable; and the one person in her house who was nearer to her own level, who was her companion and most important minister, was very comfortable too. This was a young woman about twenty, a very distant relation, with "no claim," everybody said, upon her kind mistress and friend,--the daughter of a distant cousin. How very few think anything at all of such a tie! but Lady Mary had taken her young namesake when she was a child, and she had grown up as it were at her godmother's footstool, in the conviction that the measured existence of the old was the rule of life, and that her own trifling personality counted for nothing, or next to nothing, in its steady progress. Her name was Mary too--always called "little Mary" as having once been little, and not yet very much in the matter of size. She was one of the pleasantest things to look at of all the pretty things in Lady Mary's rooms, and she had the most sheltered, peaceful, and pleasant life that could be conceived. The only little thorn in her pillow was, that whereas in the novels, of which she read a great many, the heroines all go and pay visits and have adventures, she had none, but lived constantly at home. There was something much more serious in her life, had she known, which was that she had nothing, and no power of doing anything for herself; that she had all her life been accustomed to a modest luxury which would make poverty very hard to her; and that Lady Mary was over eighty, and had made no will. If she did not make any will, her property would all go to her grandson, who was so rich already that her fortune would be but as a drop in the ocean to him; or to some great-grandchildren of whom she knew very little,--the descendants of a daughter long ago dead who had married an Austrian, and who were therefore foreigners both in birth and name. That she should provide for little Mary was therefore a thing which nature demanded, and which would hurt nobody. She had said so often; but she deferred the doing of it as a thing for which there was no hurry. For why should she die? There seemed no reason or need for it. So long as she lived, nothing could be more sure, more happy and serene, than little Mary's life; and why should she die? She did not perhaps put this into words; but the meaning of her smile, and the manner in which she put aside every suggestion about the chances of the hereafter away from her, said it more clearly than words. It was not that she had any superstitious fear about the making of a will. When the doctor or the vicar or her man of business, the only persons who ever talked to her on the subject, ventured periodically to refer to it, she assented pleasantly,--yes, certainly, she must do it--some time or other.

"It is a very simple thing to do," the lawyer said. "I will save you all trouble; nothing but your signature will be wanted--and that you give every day."

"Oh, I should think nothing of the trouble!" she said.

"And it would liberate your mind from all care, and leave you free to think of things more important still," said the clergyman.

"I think I am very free of care," she replied.

Then the doctor added bluntly, "And you will not die an hour the sooner for having made your will."

"Die!" said Lady Mary, surprised. And then she added, with a smile, "I hope you don't think so little of me as to believe I would be kept back by that?"

These gentlemen all consulted together in despair, and asked each other what should be done. They thought her an egotist--a cold-hearted old woman, holding at arm's length any idea of the inevitable. And so she did; but not because she was cold-hearted,--because she was so accustomed to living, and had survived so many calamities, and gone on so long--so long; and because everything was so comfortably arranged about her--all her little habits so firmly established, as if nothing could interfere with them. To think of the day arriving which should begin with some other formula than that of her maid's entrance drawing aside the curtains, lighting the cheerful fire, bringing her a report of the weather; and then the little tray, resplendent with snowy linen and shining silver and china, with its bouquet of violets or a rose in the season, the newspaper carefully dried and cut, the letters,--every detail was so perfect, so unchanging, regular as the morning. It seemed impossible that it should come to an end. And then when she came downstairs, there were all the little articles upon her table always ready to her hand; a certain number of things to do, each at the appointed hour; the slender refreshments it was necessary for her to take, in which there was a little exquisite variety--but never any change in the fact that at eleven and at three and so forth something had to be taken. Had a woman wanted to abandon the peaceful life which was thus supported and carried on, the very framework itself would have resisted. It was impossible (almost) to contemplate the idea that at a given moment the whole machinery must stop. She was neither without heart nor without religion, but on the contrary a good woman, to whom many gentle thoughts had been given at various portions of her career. But the occasion seemed to have passed for that as well as other kinds of emotion. The mere fact of living was enough for her. The little exertion which it was well she was required to make produced a pleasant weariness. It was a duty much enforced upon her by all around her, that she should do nothing which would exhaust or fatigue. "I don't want you to think," even the doctor would say; "you have done enough of thinking in your time." And this she accepted with great composure of spirit. She had thought and felt and done much in her day; but now everything of the kind was over. There was no need for her to fatigue herself; and day followed day, all warm and sheltered and pleasant. People died, it is true, now and then, out of doors; but they were mostly young people, whose death might have been prevented had proper care been taken,--who were seized with violent maladies, or caught sudden infections, or were cut down by accident; all which things seemed natural. Her own contemporaries were very few, and they were like herself--living on in something of the same way. At eighty-five all people under seventy are young; and one's contemporaries are very, very few.

Nevertheless these men did disturb her a little about her will. She had made more than one will in the former days during her active life; but all those to whom she had bequeathed her possessions were dead. She had survived them all, and inherited from many of them; which had been a hard thing in its time. One day the lawyer had been more than ordinarily pressing. He had told her stories of men who had died intestate, and left trouble and penury behind them to those whom they would have most wished to preserve from all trouble. It would not have become Mr. Furnival to say brutally to Lady Mary, "This is how you will leave your godchild when you die." But he told her story after story, many of them piteous enough.

"People think it is so troublesome a business," he said, "when it is nothing at all--the most easy matter in the world. We are getting so much less particular nowadays about formalities. So long as the testator's intentions are made quite apparent--that is the chief matter, and a very bad thing for us lawyers."

"I dare say," said Lady Mary, "it is unpleasant for a man to think of himself as 'the testator.' It is a very abstract title, when you come to think of it."

"Pooh'" said Mr. Furnival, who had no sense of humor.

"But if this great business is so very simple," she went on, "one could do it, no doubt, for one's self?"

"Many people do, but it is never advisable," said the lawyer. "You will say it is natural for me to tell you that. When they do, it should be as simple as possible. I give all my real property, or my personal property, or my share in so-and-so, or my jewels, or so forth, to--whoever it may be. The fewer words the better,--so that nobody may be able to read between the lines, you know,--and the signature attested by two witnesses; but they must not be witnesses that have any interest; that is, that have anything left to them by the document they witness."

Lady Mary put up her hand defensively, with a laugh. It was still a most deli-cate hand, like ivory, a little yellowed with age, but fine, the veins standing out a little upon it, the finger-tips still pink. "You speak," she said, "as if you expected me to take the law in my own hands. No, no, my old friend; never fear, you shall have the doing of it."

"Whenever you please, my dear lady--whenever you please. Such a thing can-not be done an hour too soon. Shall I take your instructions now?"

Lady Mary laughed, and said, "You were always a very keen man for business. I remember your father used to say, Robert would never neglect an opening."

"No," he said, with a peculiar look. "I have always looked after my six-and-eightpences; and in that case it is true, the pounds take care of themselves."

"Very good care," said Lady Mary; and then she bade her young companion bring that book she had been reading, where there was something she wanted to show Mr. Furnival. "It is only a case in a novel, but I am sure it is bad law; give me your opinion," she said.

He was obliged to be civil, very civil. Nobody is rude to the Lady Marys of life; and besides, she was old enough to have an additional right to every courtesy. But while he sat over the novel, and tried with unnecessary vehemence to make her see what very bad law it was, and glanced from her smiling attention to the innocent sweetness of the girl beside her, who was her loving attendant, the good man's heart was sore. He said many hard things of her in his own mind as he went away.

"She will die," he said bitterly. "She will go off in a moment when nobody is looking for it, and that poor child will be left destitute."

It was all he could do not to go back and take her by her fragile old shoulders and force her to sign and seal at once. But then he knew very well that as soon as he found himself in her presence, he would of necessity be obliged to subdue his impatience, and be once more civil, very civil, and try to suggest and insinuate the duty which he dared not force upon her. And it was very clear that till she pleased she would take no hint. He supposed it must be that strange reluctance to part with their power which is said to be common to old people, or else that horror of death, and determination to keep it at arm's length, which is also common. Thus he did as spectators are so apt to do, he forced a meaning and motive into what had no mo-

tive at all, and imagined Lady Mary, the kindest of women, to be of purpose and
intention risking the future of the girl whom she had brought up, and whom she
loved,--not with passion, indeed, or anxiety, but with tender benevolence; a theory
which was as false as anything could be.

That evening in her room, Lady Mary, in a very cheerful mood, sat by a little
bright unnecessary fire, with her writing-book before her, waiting till she should
be sleepy. It was the only point in which she was a little hard upon her maid, who
in every other respect was the best-treated of servants. Lady Mary, as it happened,
had often no inclination for bed till the night was far advanced. She slept little, as is
common enough at her age. She was in her warm wadded dressing-gown, an article
in which she still showed certain traces (which were indeed visible in all she wore)
of her ancient beauty, with her white hair becomingly arranged under a cap of cam-
bric and lace. At the last moment, when she had been ready to step into bed, she
had changed her mind, and told Jervis that she would write a letter or two first. And
she had written her letters, but still felt no inclination to sleep. Then there fluttered
across her memory somehow the conversation she had held with Mr. Furnival in
the morning. It would be amusing, she thought, to cheat him out of some of those
six-and-eightpences he pretended to think so much of. It would be still more amusing, next time the subject of her will was recurred to, to give his arm a little tap with
her fan, and say, "Oh, that is all settled, months ago." She laughed to herself at this,
and took out a fresh sheet of paper. It was a little jest that pleased her.

"Do you think there is any one up yet, Jervis, except you and me?" she said to
the maid. Jervis hesitated a little, and then said that she believed Mr. Brown had not
gone to bed yet; for he had been going over the cellar, and was making up his ac-
counts. Jervis was so explanatory that her mistress divined what was meant. "I suppose I have been spoiling sport, keeping you here," she said good-humoredly; for it
was well known that Miss Jervis and Mr. Brown were engaged, and that they were
only waiting (everybody knew but Lady Mary, who never suspected it) the death of
their mistress, to set up a lodging-house in Jermyn Street, where they fully intended
to make their fortune. "Then go," Lady Mary said, "and call Brown. I have a little
business paper to write, and you must both witness my signature." She laughed to
herself a little as she said this, thinking how she would steal a march on Mr. Furnival. "I give, and bequeath," she said to herself playfully, after Jervis had hurried

away. She fully intended to leave both of these good servants something, but then she recollected that people who are interested in a will cannot sign as witnesses. "What does it matter?" she said to herself gayly; "If it ever should be wanted, Mary would see to that." Accordingly she dashed off, in her pretty, old-fashioned handwriting, which was very angular and pointed, as was the fashion in her day, and still very clear, though slightly tremulous, a few lines, in which, remembering playfully Mr. Furnival's recommendation of "few words," she left to little Mary all she possessed, adding, by the prompting of that recollection about the witnesses, "She will take care of the servants." It filled one side only of the large sheet of notepaper, which was what Lady Mary habitually used. Brown, introduced timidly by Jervis, and a little overawed by the solemnity of the bedchamber, came in and painted solidly his large signature after the spidery lines of his mistress. She had folded down the paper, so that neither saw what it was.

"Now I will go to bed," Lady Mary said, when Brown had left the room. "And Jervis, you must go to bed too."

"Yes, my lady," said Jervis.

"I don't approve of courtship at this hour."

"No, my lady," Jervis replied, deprecating and disappointed.

"Why cannot he tell his tale in daylight?"

"Oh, my lady, there's no tale to tell," cried the maid. "We are not of the gossiping sort, my lady, neither me nor Mr. Brown." Lady Mary laughed, and watched while the candles were put out, the fire made a pleasant flicker in the room,--it was autumn and still warm, and it was "for company" and cheerfulness that the little fire was lit; she liked to see it dancing and flickering upon the walls,--and then closed her eyes amid an exquisite softness of comfort and luxury, life itself bearing her up as softly, filling up all the crevices as warmly, as the downy pillow upon which she rested her still beautiful old head.

If she had died that night! The little sheet of paper that meant so much lay openly, innocently, in her writing-book, along with the letters she had written, and looking of as little importance as they. There was nobody in the world who grudged old Lady Mary one of those pretty placid days of hers. Brown and Jervis, if they were sometimes a little impatient, consoled each other that they were both sure of something in her will, and that in the mean time it was a very good place. And all the rest would have been very well content that Lady Mary should live forever. But how wonderfully it would have simplified everything, and how much trouble and pain it would have saved to everybody, herself included, could she have died that night!

But naturally, there was no question of dying on that night. When she was about to go downstairs, next day, Lady Mary, giving her letters to be posted, saw the paper she had forgotten lying beside them. She had forgotten all about it, but the sight of it made her smile. She folded it up and put it in an envelope while Jervis went down-stairs with the letters; and then, to carry out her joke, she looked round her to see where she would put it. There was an old Italian cabinet in the room, with a secret drawer, which it was a little difficult to open,--almost impossible for any one who did not know the secret. Lady Mary looked round her, smiled, hesitated a little, and then walked across the room and put the envelope in the secret drawer. She was still fumbling with it when Jervis came back; but there was no connection in Jervis's mind, then or ever after, between the paper she had signed and this old cabinet, which was one of the old lady's toys. She arranged Lady Mary's shawl, which had dropped off her shoulders a little in her unusual activity, and took up her book and her favorite cushion, and all the little paraphernalia that moved with her, and gave her lady her arm to go down-stairs; where little Mary had placed her chair just at the right angle, and arranged the little table, on which there were so many little necessaries and conveniences, and was standing smiling, the prettiest object of all, the climax of the gentle luxury and pleasantness, to receive her god-mother, who had been her providence all her life.

But what a pity! oh, what a pity, that she had not died that night!

II.

Life went on after this without any change. There was never any change in that delightful house; and if it was years, or months, or even days, the youngest of its inhabitants could scarcely tell, and Lady Mary could not tell at all. This was one of her little imperfections,--a little mist which hung, like the lace about her head, over her memory. She could not remember how time went, or that there was any difference between one day and another. There were Sundays, it was true, which made a kind of gentle measure of the progress of time; but she said, with a smile, that she thought it was always Sunday--they came so close upon each other. And time flew on gentle wings, that made no sound and left no reminders. She had her little ailments like anybody, but in reality less than anybody, seeing there was nothing to fret her, nothing to disturb the even tenor of her days. Still there were times when she took a little cold, or got a chill, in spite of all precautions, as she went from one room to another. She came to be one of the marvels of the time,--an old lady who had seen everybody worth seeing for generations back; who remembered as distinctly as if they had happened yesterday, great events that had taken place before the present age began at all, before the great statesmen of our time were born; and in full possession of all her faculties, as everybody said, her mind as clear as ever, her intelligence as active, reading everything, interested in everything, and still beautiful, in extreme old age. Everybody about her, and in particular all the people who helped to keep the thorns from her path, and felt themselves to have a hand in her preservation, were proud of Lady Mary and she was perhaps a little, a very little, delightfully, charmingly, proud of herself. The doctor, beguiled by professional vanity, feeling what a feather she was in his cap, quite confident that she would reach her hundredth birthday, and with an ecstatic hope that even, by grace of his admirable treatment and her own beautiful constitution, she might (almost) solve the problem and live forever, gave up troubling about the will which at a former period he had taken so much interest in. "What is the use?" he said; "she will see us all out." And the vicar, though he did not give in to this, was overawed by the old lady, who knew everything that could be taught her, and to whom it seemed an impertinence to utter commonplaces about duty, or even to suggest subjects of thought. Mr. Furnival was the only man who did not cease his representations, and whose anxiety about the young Mary, who was so blooming and sweet in the shadow of the old, did not decrease. But the recollection of the bit of paper in the secret drawer of the cabinet, fortified his old client against all his attacks. She had intended it only as a jest, with which some day or other to confound him, and show how much wiser she was than he supposed. It became quite a pleasant subject of thought to her, at which she laughed to herself. Some day, when she had a suitable moment, she would order him to come with all his formalities, and then produce her bit of paper, and turn the laugh against him. But oddly, the very existence of that little document kept her indifferent even to the laugh. It was too much trouble; she only smiled at him, and took no more notice, amused to think how astonished he would be,--when, if ever, he found it out.

It happened, however, that one day in the early winter the wind changed when Lady Mary was out for her drive; at least they all vowed the wind changed. It was in the south, that genial quarter, when she set out, but turned about in some uncomfortable way, and was a keen northeaster when she came back. And in the moment of stepping from the carriage, she caught a chill. It was the coachman's fault, Jervis said, who allowed the horses to make a step forward when Lady Mary was getting out, and kept her exposed, standing on the step of the carriage, while he pulled them up; and it was Jervis's fault, the footman said, who was not clever enough to get her lady out, or even to throw a shawl round her when she perceived how the weather had changed. It is always some one's fault, or some unforeseen, unprecedented change, that does it at the last. Lady Mary was not accustomed to be ill, and did not bear it with her usual grace. She was a little impatient at first, and thought they were making an unnecessary fuss. But then there passed a few uncomfortable feverish days, when she began to look forward to the doctor's visit as the only thing there was any comfort in. Afterwards she passed a night of a very agitating kind. She dozed and dreamed, and awoke and dreamed again. Her life seemed all to run into dreams,--a strange confusion was about her, through which she could define nothing. Once waking up, as she supposed, she saw a group round her bed, the doctor,--with a candle in his hand, (how should the doctor be there in the middle of the night?) holding her hand or feeling her pulse; little Mary at one side, crying,--why should the child cry?--and Jervis, very, anxious, pouring something into a glass. There were other faces there which she was sure must have come out of a dream,--so unlikely was it that they should be collected in her bedchamber,--and all with a sort of halo of feverish light about them; a magnified and mysterious importance. This strange scene, which she did not understand, seemed to make itself visible all in a moment out of the darkness, and then disappeared again as suddenly as it came.

III.

When she woke again, it was morning; and her first waking consciousness was, that she must be much better. The choking sensation in her throat was altogether gone. She had no desire to cough--no difficulty in breathing. She had a fancy, however, that she must be still dreaming, for she felt sure that some one had called her by her name, "Mary." Now all who could call her by her Christian name were dead years ago; therefore it must be a dream. However, in a short time it was repeated,--"Mary, Mary! get up; there is a great deal to do." This voice confused her greatly. Was it possible that all that was past had been mere fancy, that she had but dreamed those long, long years,--maturity and motherhood, and trouble and triumph, and old age at the end of all? It seemed to her possible that she might have dreamed the rest,--for she had been a girl much given to visions,--but she said to herself that she never could have dreamed old age. And then with a smile she mused, and thought that it must be the voice that was a dream; for how could she get up without Jervis, who had never appeared yet to draw the curtains or make the fire? Jervis perhaps had sat up late. She remembered now to have seen her that time in the middle of the night by her bedside; so that it was natural enough, poor thing, that she should be late. Get up! who was it that was calling to her so? She had not been so called to, she who had always been a great lady, since she was a girl by her mother's side. "Mary, Mary!" It was a very curious dream. And what was more curious still was, that by-and-by she could not keep still any longer, but got up without thinking any more of Jervis, and going out of her room came all at once into the midst of a company of people, all very busy; whom she was much surprised to find, at first, but whom she soon accustomed herself to, finding the greatest interest in their proceedings, and curious to know what they were doing. They, for their part, did not seem at all surprised by her appearance, nor did any one stop to explain, as would have been natural; but she took this with great composure, somewhat astonished, perhaps, being used, wherever she went, to a great many observances and much respect, but soon, very soon, becoming used to it. Then some one repeated what she had heard before. "It is time you got up,--for there is a great deal to do."

"To do," she said, "for me?" and then she looked round upon them with that charming smile which had subjugated so many. "I am afraid," she said, "you will find me of very little use. I am too old now, if ever I could have done much, for work."

"Oh no, you are not old,--you will do very well," some one said.

"Not old!"--Lady Mary felt a little offended in spite of herself. "Perhaps I like flattery as well as my neighbors," she said with dignity, "but then it must be reasonable. To say I am anything but a very old woman--"

Here she paused a little, perceiving for the first time, with surprise, that she was standing and walking without her stick or the help of any one's arm, quite freely and at her ease, and that the place in which she was had expanded into a great place like a gallery in a palace, instead of the room next her own into which she had walked a few minutes ago; but this discovery did not at all affect her mind, or occupy her except with the most passing momentary surprise.

"The fact is, I feel a great deal better and stronger," she said.

"Quite well, Mary, and stronger than ever you were before?"

"Who is it that calls me Mary? I have had nobody for a long time to call me Mary; the friends of my youth are all dead. I think that you must be right, although the doctor, I feel sure, thought me very bad last night. I should have got alarmed if I had not fallen asleep again."

"And then woke up well?"

"Quite well: it is wonderful, but quite true. You seem to know a great deal about me."

"I know everything about you. You have had a very pleasant life, and do you think you have made the best of it? Your old age has been very pleasant."

"Ah! you acknowledge that I am old, then?" cried Lady Mary with a smile.

"You are old no longer, and you are a great lady no longer. Don't you see that something has happened to you? It is seldom that such a great change happens without being found out."

"Yes; it is true I have got better all at once. I feel an extraordinary renewal of strength. I seem to have left home without knowing it; none of my people seem near me. I feel very much as if I had just awakened from a long dream. Is it possible," she said, with a wondering look, "that I have dreamed all my life, and after all am just a girl at home?" The idea was ludicrous, and she laughed. "You see I am very much improved indeed," she said.

She was still so far from perceiving the real situation, that some one came towards her out of the group of people about--some one whom she recognized--with the evident intention of explaining to her how it was. She started a little at the sight of him, and held out her hand, and cried: "You here! I am very glad to see you--doubly glad, since I was told a few days ago that you had--died."

There was something in this word as she herself pronounced it that troubled her a little. She had never been one of those who are afraid of death. On the contrary, she had always taken a great interest in it, and liked to hear everything that could be told her on the subject. It gave her now, however, a curious little thrill of sensation, which she did not understand: she hoped it was not superstition.

"You have guessed rightly," he said, "quite right. That is one of the words with a false meaning, which is to us a mere symbol of something we cannot understand. But you see what it means now."

It was a great shock, it need not be concealed. Otherwise, she had been quite pleasantly occupied with the interest of something new, into which she had walked so easily out of her own bedchamber, without any trouble, and with the delightful new sensation of health and strength. But when it flashed upon her that she was not to go back to her bedroom again, nor have any of those cares and attentions which had seemed necessary to existence, she was very much startled and shaken. Died? Was it possible that she personally had died? She had known it was a thing that happened to everybody; but yet--And it was a solemn matter, to be prepared for, and looked forward to, whereas--"If you mean that I too--" she said, faltering a little; and then she added, "it is very surprising," with a trouble in her mind which yet was not all trouble. "If that is so, it is a thing well over. And it is very wonderful how much disturbance people give themselves about it--if this is all."

"This is not all, however," her friend said; "you have an ordeal before you which you will not find pleasant. You are going to think about your life, and all that was imperfect in it, and which might have been done better."

"We are none of us perfect," said Lady Mary, with a little of that natural resentment with which one hears one's self accused,--however ready one may be to accuse one's self.

"Permit me," said he, and took her hand and led her away without further explanation. The people about were so busy with their own occupations that they took very little notice; neither did she pay much attention to the manner in which they were engaged. Their looks were friendly when they met her eye, and she too felt friendly, with a sense of brotherhood. But she had always been a kind woman. She wanted to step aside and help, on more than one occasion, when it seemed to her that some people in her way had a task above their powers; but this her conductor would not permit. And she endeavored to put some questions to him as they went along, with still less success.

"The change is very confusing," she said; "one has no standard to judge by. I should like to know something about--the kind of people--and the--manner of life."

"For a time," he said, "you will have enough to do, without troubling yourself about that."

This naturally produced an uneasy sensation in her mind. "I suppose," she said, rather timidly, "that we are not in--what we have been accustomed to call heaven?"

"That is a word," he said, "which expresses rather a condition than a place."

"But there must be a place--in which that condition can exist." She had always been fond of discussions of this kind, and felt encouraged to find that they were still practicable. "It cannot be the--Inferno; that is clear, at least," she added, with the sprightliness which was one of her characteristics; "perhaps--Purgatory? since you infer I have something to endure."

"Words are interchangeable," he said: "that means one thing to one of us which to another has a totally different signification." There was something so like his old self in this, that she laughed with an irresistible sense of amusement.

"You were always fond of the oracular," she said. She was conscious that on former occasions, if he made such a speech to her, though she would have felt the same amusement, she would not have expressed it so frankly. But he did not take it at all amiss. And her thoughts went on in other directions. She felt herself saying over to herself the words of the old north-country dirge, which came to her recollection she knew not how--

If hosen and shoon thou gavest nane, The whins shall prick thee intil the bane.

When she saw that her companion heard her, she asked, "Is that true?"

He shook his head a little. "It is too matter of fact," he said, "as I need hardly tell you. Hosen and shoon are good, but they do not always sufficiently indicate the state of the heart."

Lady Mary had a consciousness, which was pleasant to her, that so far as the hosen and shoon went, she had abundant means of preparing herself for the pricks of any road, however rough; but she had no time to indulge this pleasing reflection, for she was shortly introduced into a great building, full of innumerable rooms, in one of which her companion left her.

IV.

The door opened, and she felt herself free to come out. How long she had been there, or what passed there, is not for any one to say. She came out tingling and smarting--if such words can be used--with an intolerable recollection of the last act of her life. So intolerable was it that all that had gone before, and all the risings up of old errors and visions long dead, were forgotten in the sharp and keen prick of this, which was not over and done like the rest. No one had accused her, or brought before her judge the things that were against her. She it was who had done it all,--she, whose memory did not spare her one fault, who remembered everything. But when she came to that last frivolity of her old age, and saw for the first time how she had played with the future of the child whom she had brought up, and abandoned to the hardest fate,--for nothing, for folly, for a jest,--the horror and bitterness of the thought filled her mind to overflowing. In the first anguish of that recollection she had to go forth, receiving no word of comfort in respect to it, meeting only with a look of sadness and compassion, which went to her very heart. She came forth as if she had been driven away, but not by any outward influence, by the force of her own miserable sensations. "I will write," she said to herself, "and tell them; I will go--" And then she stopped short, remembering that she could neither go nor write,--that all communication with the world she had left was closed. Was it all closed? Was there no way in which a message could reach those who remained behind? She caught the first passer-by whom she passed, and addressed him piteously. "Oh, tell me,--you have been longer here than I,--cannot one send a letter, a message, if it were only a single word?"

"Where?" he said, stopping and listening; so that it began to seem possible to her that some such expedient might still be within her reach.

"It is to England," she said, thinking he meant to ask as to which quarter of the world.

"Ah," he said, shaking his head, "I fear that it is impossible."

"But it is to set something right, which out of mere inadvertence, with no ill meaning,"--No, no (she repeated to herself), no ill-meaning--none! "Oh sir, for charity! tell me how I can find a way. There must--there must be some way."

He was greatly moved by the sight of her distress. "I am but a stranger here," he said; "I may be wrong. There are others who can tell you better; but"--and he shook his head sadly--"most of us would be so thankful, if we could, to send a word, if it were only a single word, to those we have left behind, that I fear, I fear--"

"Ah!" cried Lady Mary, "but that would be only for the tenderness; whereas this is for justice and for pity, and to do away with a great wrong which I did before I came here."

"I am very sorry for you," he said; but shook his head once more as he went away. She was more careful next time, and chose one who had the look of much experience and knowledge of the place. He listened to her very gravely, and answered yes, that he was one of the officers, and could tell her whatever she wanted to know; but when she told him what she wanted, he too shook his head. "I do not say it cannot be done," he said. "There are some cases in which it has been successful, but very few. It has often been attempted. There is no law against it. Those who do it do it at their own risk. They suffer much, and almost always they fail."

"No, oh no! You said there were some who succeeded. No one can be more anxious than I. I will give--anything--everything I have in the world!"

He gave her a smile, which was very grave nevertheless, and full of pity. "You forget," he said, "that you have nothing to give; and if you had, that there is no one here to whom it would be of any value."

Though she was no longer old and weak, yet she was still a woman, and she began to weep, in the terrible failure and contrariety of all things; but yet she would not yield. She cried: "There must be some one here who would do it for love. I have had people who loved me in my time. I must have some here who have not forgotten me. Ah! I know what you would say. I lived so long I forgot them all, and why should they remember me?"

Here she was touched on the arm, and looking round, saw close to her the face of one whom, it was very true, she had forgotten. She remembered him but dimly after she had looked long at him. A little group had gathered about her, with grieved looks, to see her distress. He who had touched her was the spokesman of them all.

"There is nothing I would not do," he said, "for you and for love." And then they all sighed, surrounding her, and added, "But it is impossible--impossible!"

She stood and gazed at them, recognizing by degrees faces that she knew, and seeing in all that look of grief and sympathy which makes all human souls brothers. Impossible was not a word that had been often said to be in her life; and to come out of a world in which everything could be changed, everything communicated in the twinkling of an eye, and find a dead blank before her and around her, through which not a word could go, was more terrible than can be said in words. She looked piteously upon them, with that anguish of helplessness which goes to every heart, and cried, "What is impossible? To send a word--only a word--to set right what is wrong? Oh, I understand," she said, lifting up her hands. "I understand that to send messages of comfort must not be; that the people who love you must bear it, as we all have done in our time, and trust to God for consolation. But I have done a wrong! Oh, listen, listen to me, my friends. I have left a child, a young creature, unprovided for--without any one to help her. And must that be? Must she bear it, and I bear it, forever, and no means, no way of setting it right? Listen to me! I was there last night,--in the middle of the night I was still there,--and here this morning. So it must be easy to come--only a short way; and two words would be enough,--only two words!"

They gathered closer and closer round her, full of compassion. "It is easy to come," they said, "but not to go."

And one added, "It will not be forever; comfort yourself. When she comes here, or to a better place, that will seem to you only as a day.

"But to her," cried Lady Mary,--"to her it will be long years--it will be trouble and sorrow; and she will think I took no thought for her; and she will be right," the penitent said with a great and bitter cry.

It was so terrible that they were all silent, and said not a word,--except the man who had loved her, who put his hand upon her arm, and said, "We are here for that; this is the fire that purges us,--to see at last what we have done, and the true aspect of it, and to know the cruel wrong, yet never be able to make amends."

She remembered then that this was a man who had neglected all lawful affections, and broken the hearts of those who trusted him for her sake; and for a moment she forgot her own burden in sorrow for his.

It was now that he who had called himself one of the officers came forward again; for the little crowd had gathered round her so closely that he had been shut out. He said, "No one can carry your message for you; that is not permitted. But there is still a possibility. You may have permission to go yourself. Such things have been done, though they have not often been successful. But if you will--"

She shivered when she heard him; and it became apparent to her why no one could be found to go,--for all her nature revolted from that step, which it was evident must be the most terrible which could be thought of. She looked at him with troubled, beseeching eyes, and the rest all looked at her, pitying and trying to soothe her.

"Permission will not be refused," he said, "for a worthy cause."

Upon which the others all spoke together, entreating her. "Already," they cried, "they have forgotten you living. You are to them one who is dead. They will be afraid of you if they can see you. Oh, go not back! Be content to wait,--to wait; it is only a little while. The life of man is nothing; it appears for a little time, and then it vanishes away. And when she comes here she will know,--or in a better place." They sighed as they named the better place; though some smiled too, feeling perhaps more near to it.

Lady Mary listened to them all, but she kept her eyes upon the face of him who offered her this possibility. There passed through her mind a hundred stories she had heard of those who had **gone back**. But not one that spoke of them as welcome, as received with joy, as comforting those they loved. Ah no! was it not rather a curse upon the house to which they came? The rooms were shut up, the houses abandoned, where they were supposed to appear. Those whom they had loved best feared and fled them. They were a vulgar wonder,--a thing that the poorest laughed at, yet feared. Poor, banished souls! it was because no one would listen to them that they had to linger and wait, and come and go. She shivered, and in spite of her longing and her repentance, a cold dread and horror took possession of her. She looked round upon her companions for comfort, and found none.

"Do not go," they said; "do not go. We have endured like you. We wait till all things are made clear."

And another said, "All will be made clear. It is but for a time."

She turned from one to another, and back again to the first speaker,--he who had authority.

He said, "It is very rarely successful; it retards the course of your penitence. It is an indulgence, and it may bring harm and not good but if the meaning is generous and just, permission will be given, and you may go."

Then all the strength of her nature rose in her. She thought of the child forsaken, and of the dark world round her, where she would find so few friends; and of the home shut up in which she had lived her young and pleasant life; and of the thoughts that must rise in her heart, as though she were forsaken and abandoned of God and man. Then Lady Mary turned to the man who had authority. She said, "If he whom I saw to-day will give me his blessing, I will go--" and they all pressed round her, weeping and kissing her hands.

"He will not refuse his blessing," they said; "but the way is terrible, and you are still weak. How can you encounter all the misery of it? He commands no one to try that dark and dreadful way."

"I will try," Lady Mary said.

V.

The night which Lady Mary had been conscious of, in a momentary glimpse full of the exaggeration of fever, had not indeed been so expeditious as she believed. The doctor, it is true, had been pronouncing her death-warrant when she saw him holding her wrist, and wondered what he did there in the middle of the night; but she had been very ill before this, and the conclusion of her life had been watched with many tears. Then there had risen up a wonderful commotion in the house, of which little Mary, her godchild, was very little sensible. Had she left any will, any instructions, the slightest indication of what she wished to be done after her death? Mr. Furnival, who had been very anxious to be allowed to see her, even in the last days of her illness, said emphatically, no. She had never executed any will, never made any disposition of her affairs, he said, almost with bitterness, in the tone of one who is ready to weep with vexation and distress. The vicar took a more hopeful view. He said it was impossible that so considerate a person could have done this, and that there must, he was sure, be found somewhere, if close examination was made, a memorandum, a letter,--something which should show what she wished; for she must have known very well, notwithstanding all flatteries and compliments upon her good looks, that from day to day her existence was never to be calculated upon. The doctor did not share this last opinion. He said that there was no fathoming the extraordinary views that people took of their own case; and that it was quite possible, though it seemed incredible, that Lady Mary might really be as little expectant of death, on the way to ninety, as a girl of seventeen; but still he was of opinion that she might have left a memorandum somewhere.

These three gentlemen were in the foreground of affairs; because she had no relations to step in and take the management. The earl, her grandson, was abroad, and there were only his solicitors to interfere on his behalf, men to whom Lady

Mary's fortune was quite unimportant, although it was against their principles to let anything slip out of their hands that could aggrandize their client; but who knew nothing about the circumstances,--about little Mary, about the old lady's peculiarities, in any way. Therefore the persons who had surrounded her in her life, and Mr. Furnival, her man of business, were the persons who really had the management of everything. Their wives interfered a little too, or rather the one wife who only could do so,--the wife of the vicar, who came in beneficently at once, and took poor little Mary, in her first desolation, out of the melancholy house. Mrs. Vicar did this without any hesitation, knowing very well that, in all probability, Lady Mary had made no will, and consequently that the poor girl was destitute. A great deal is said about the hardness of the world, and the small consideration that is shown for a destitute dependent in such circumstances. But this is not true; and, as a matter of fact, there is never, or very rarely, such profound need in the world, without a great deal of kindness and much pity. The three gentlemen all along had been entirely in Mary's interest. They had not expected legacies from the old lady, or any advantage to themselves. It was of the girl that they had thought. And when now they examined everything and inquired into all her ways and what she had done, it was of Mary they were thinking. But Mr. Furnival was very certain of his point. He knew that Lady Mary had made no will; time after time he had pressed it upon her. He was very sure, even while he examined her writing-table, and turned out all the drawers, that nothing would be found. The little Italian cabinet had *chiffons* in its drawers, fragments of old lace, pieces of ribbon, little nothings of all sorts. Nobody thought of the secret drawer; and if they had thought of it, where could a place have been found less likely? If she had ever made a will, she could have had no reason for concealing it. To be sure, they did not reason in this way, being simply unaware of any place of concealment at all. And Mary knew nothing about this search they were making. She did not know how she was herself "left." When the first misery of grief was exhausted, she began, indeed, to have troubled thoughts in her own mind,--to expect that the vicar would speak to her, or Mr. Furnival send for her, and tell her what she was to do. But nothing was said to her. The vicar's wife had asked her to come for a long visit; and the anxious people, who were forever talking over this subject and consulting what was best for her, had come to no decision as yet, as to what must be said to the person chiefly concerned. It was too heart-rending to have to put the real state of affairs before her.

The doctor had no wife; but he had an anxious mother, who, though she would not for the world have been unkind to the poor girl, yet was very anxious that she should be disposed of and out of her son's way. It is true that the doctor was forty and Mary only eighteen,--but what then? Matches of that kind were seen every day; and his heart was so soft to the child that his mother never knew from one day to another what might happen. She had naturally no doubt at all that Mary would seize the first hand held out to her; and as time went on, held many an anxious consultation with the vicar's wife on the subject. "You cannot have her with you forever," she said. "She must know one time or another how she is left, and that she must learn to do something for herself."

"Oh," said the vicar's wife, "how is she to be told? It is heart-rending to look at her and to think,--nothing but luxury all her life, and now, in a moment, destitution. I am very glad to have her with me: she is a dear little thing, and so nice with the children. And if some good man would only step in--"

The doctor's mother trembled; for that a good man should step in was exactly what she feared. "That is a thing that can never be depended upon," she said; "and marriages made out of compassion are just as bad as mercenary marriages. Oh no, my dear Mrs. Bowyer, Mary has a great deal of character. You should put more confidence in her than that. No doubt she will be much cast down at first, but when she knows, she will rise to the occasion and show what is in her."

"Poor little thing! what is in a girl of eighteen, and one that has lain on the roses and fed on the lilies all her life? Oh, I could find it in my heart to say a great deal about old Lady Mary that would not be pleasant! Why did she bring her up so if she did not mean to provide for her? I think she must have been at heart a wicked old woman."

"Oh no! we must not say that. I dare say, as my son says, she always meant to do it sometime-"

"Sometime! how long did she expect to live, I wonder?"

"Well," said the doctor's mother, "it is wonderful how little old one feels sometimes within one's self, even when one is well up in years." She was of the faction of the old, instead of being like Mrs. Bowyer, who was not much over thirty, of the faction of the young. She could make excuses for Lady Mary; but she thought that it was unkind to bring the poor little girl here in ignorance of her real position, and in the way of men who, though old enough to know better, were still capable of folly,--as what man is not, when a girl of eighteen is concerned? "I hope," she added, "that the earl will do something for her. Certainly he ought to, when he knows all that his grandmother did, and what her intentions must have been. He ought to make her a little allowance; that is the least he can do,--not, to be sure, such a provision as we all hoped Lady Mary was going to make for her, but enough to live upon. Mr. Furnival, I believe, has written to him to that effect."

"Hush!" cried the vicar's wife; indeed she had been making signs to the other lady, who stood with her back to the door, for some moments. Mary had come in while this conversation was going on. She had not paid any attention to it; and yet her ear had been caught by the names of Lady Mary, and the earl, and Mr. Furnival. For whom was it that the earl should make an allowance enough to live upon? whom Lady Mary had not provided for, and whom Mr. Furnival had written about? When she sat down to the needle-work in which she was helping Mrs. Vicar, it was not to be supposed that she should not ponder these words,--for some time very vaguely, not perceiving the meaning of them; and then with a start she woke up to perceive that there must be something meant, some one,--even some one she knew. And then the needle dropped out of the girl's hand, and the pinafore she was making fell on the floor. Some one! it must be herself they meant! Who but she could be the subject of that earnest conversation? She began to remember a great many conversations as earnest, which had been stopped when she came into the room, and the looks of pity which had been bent upon her. She had thought in her innocence that this was because she had lost her godmother, her protectress,--and had been very grateful for the kindness of her friends. But now another meaning came into everything. Mrs. Bowyer had accompanied her visitor to the door, still talking, and when she returned her face was very grave. But she smiled when she met Mary's look, and said cheerfully,--

"How kind of you, my dear, to make all those pinafores for me! The little ones will not know themselves. They never were so fine before."

"Oh, Mrs. Bowyer," cried the girl, "I have guessed something! and I want you to tell me! Are you keeping me for charity, and is it I that am left--without any provision, and that Mr. Furnival has written--"

She could not finish her sentence, for it was very bitter to her, as may be supposed.

"I don't know what you mean, my dear," cried the vicar's wife. "Charity,--well, I suppose that is the same as love,--at least it is so in the 13th chapter of 1st Corinthians. You are staying with us, I hope, for love, if that is what you mean."

Upon which she took the girl in her arms and kissed her, and cried, as women must. "My dearest," she said, "as you have guessed the worst, it is better to tell you. Lady Mary--I don't know why; oh, I don't wish to blame her--has left no will; and, my dear, my dear, you who have been brought up in luxury, you have not a penny." Here the vicar's wife gave Mary a closer hug, and kissed her once more. "We love you all the better,--if that was possible," she said.

How many thoughts will fly through a girl's mind while her head rests on some kind shoulder, and she is being consoled for the first calamity that has touched her life! She was neither ungrateful nor unresponsive; but as Mrs. Bowyer pressed her close to her kind breast and cried over her, Mary did not cry, but thought,--seeing in a moment a succession of scenes, and realizing in a moment so complete a new world, that all her pain was quelled by the hurry and rush in her brain as her forces rallied to sustain her. She withdrew from her kind support after a moment, with eyes tearless and shining, the color mounting to her face, and not a sign of discouragement in her, nor yet of sentiment, though she grasped her kind friend's hands with a pressure which her innocent small fingers seemed incapable of giving. "One has read of such things--in books," she said, with a faint courageous smile; "and I suppose they happen,--in life."

"Oh, my dear, too often in life. Though how people can be so cruel, so indifferent, so careless of the happiness of those they love--"

Here Mary pressed her friend's hands till they hurt, and cried, "Not cruel, not indifferent. I cannot hear a word--"

"Well, dear, it is like you to feel so,--I knew you would; and I will not say a word. Oh, Mary, if she ever thinks of such things now--"

"I hope she will not--I hope she cannot!" cried the girl, with once more a vehement pressure of her friend's hands.

"What is that?" Mrs. Bowyer said, looking round. "It is somebody in the next room, I suppose. No, dear, I hope so too, for she would not be happy if she remembered. Mary, dry your eyes, my dear. Try not to think of this. I am sure there is some one in the next room. And you must try not to look wretched, for all our sakes--"

"Wretched!" cried Mary, springing up. "I am not wretched." And she turned with a countenance glowing and full of courage to the door. But there was no one there,--no visitor lingering in the smaller room as sometimes happened.

"I thought I heard some one come in," said the vicar's wife. "Didn't you hear something, Mary? I suppose it is because I am so agitated with all this, but I could have sworn I heard some one come in."

"There is nobody," said Mary, who, in the shock of the calamity which had so suddenly changed the world to her, was perfectly calm. She did not feel at all disposed to cry or "give way." It went to her head with a thrill of pain, which was excitement as well, like a strong stimulant suddenly applied; and she added, "I should like to go out a little, if you don't mind, just to get used to the idea."

"My dear, I will get my hat in a moment--"

"No, please. It is not unkindness; but I must think it over by myself,--by myself," Mary cried. She hurried away, while Mrs. Bowyer took another survey of the outer room, and called the servant to know who had been calling. Nobody had been calling, the maid said; but her mistress still shook her head.

"It must have been some one who does not ring, who just opens the door," she said to herself. "That is the worst of the country. It might be Mrs. Blunt, or Sophia Blackburn, or the curate, or half-a-dozen people,--and they have just gone away when they heard me crying. How could I help crying? But I wonder how much they heard, whoever it was."

VI.

It was winter, and snow was on the ground.

Lady Mary found herself on the road that led through her own village, going home. It was like a picture of a wintry night,--like one of those pictures that please the children at Christmas. A little snow sprinkled on the roofs, just enough to define them, and on the edges of the roads; every cottage window showing a ruddy glimmer in the twilight; the men coming home from their work; the children, tied up in comforters and caps, stealing in from the slides, and from the pond, where they were forbidden to go; and, in the distance, the trees of the great House standing up dark, turning the twilight into night. She had a curious enjoyment in it, simple like that of a child, and a wish to talk to some one out of the fullness of her heart. She overtook, her step being far lighter than his, one of the men going home from his work, and spoke to him, telling him with a smile not to be afraid; but he never so much as raised his head, and went plodding on with his heavy step, not knowing that she had spoken to him. She was startled by this; but said to herself, that the men were dull, that their perceptions were confused, and that it was getting dark; and went on, passing him quickly. His breath made a cloud in the air as he walked, and his heavy plodding steps sounded into the frosty night. She perceived that her own were invisible and inaudible, with a curious momentary sensation, half of pleasure, half of pain. She felt no cold, and she saw through the twilight as clearly as if it had been day. There was no fatigue or sense of weakness in her; but she had the strange, wistful feeling of an exile returning after long years, not knowing how he may find those he had left. At one of the first houses in the village there was a woman standing at her door, looking out for her children; one who knew Lady Mary well. She stopped quite cheerfully to bid her good evening, as she had done in her vigorous days, before she grew old. It was a little experiment, too. She thought it possible that Catherine would scream out, and perhaps fly from her; but surely would be easily reassured when she heard the voice she knew, and saw by her one who was no ghost, but her own kind mistress. But Catherine took no notice when she spoke; she did not so much as turn her head. Lady Mary stood by her patiently, with more and more of that wistful desire to be recognized. She put her hand timidly upon the woman's arm, who was thinking of nothing but her boys, and calling to them, straining her eyes in the fading light. "Don't be afraid, they are coming, they are safe," she said, pressing Catherine's arm. But the woman never moved. She took no notice. She called to a neighbor who was passing, to ask if she had seen the children, and the two stood and talked in the dim air, not conscious of the third who stood between them, looking from one to another, astonished, paralyzed. Lady Mary had not been prepared for this; she could not believe it even now. She repeated their names more and more anxiously, and even plucked at their sleeves to call their attention. She stood as a poor dependent sometimes stands, wistful, civil, trying to say something that will please, while they talked and took no notice; and then the neighbor passed on, and Catherine went into her house. It is hard to be left out in the cold when others go into their cheerful houses; but to be thus left outside of life, to speak and not be heard, to stand unseen, astounded, unable to secure any attention! She had thought they would be frightened, but it was not they who were frightened. A great panic seized the woman who was no more of this world. She had almost rejoiced to find herself back walking so lightly, so strongly, finding everything easy that had been so hard; and yet but a few minutes had passed, and she knew never more to be deceived, that she was no longer of this world. What if she should be condemned to wander forever among familiar places that knew her no more, appealing for a look, a word, to those who could no longer see her, or hear her cry, or know of her presence? Terror seized upon her, a chill and pang of fear beyond description. She felt an impulse to fly wildly into the dark, into the night, like a lost creature; to find again somehow, she could not tell how, the door out of which she had come, and beat upon it wildly with her hands, and implore to be taken home. For a moment she stood looking round her, lost and alone in the wide universe; no one to speak to her, no one to comfort her; outside of life altogether. Other rustic figures, slow-stepping, leisurely, at their ease, went and came, one at a time; but in this place, where every stranger was an object of curiosity, no one cast a glance at her. She was as if she had never been.

Presently she found herself entering her own house. It was all shut and silent,--not a window lighted along the whole front of the house which used to twinkle and glitter with lights. It soothed her somewhat to see this, as if in evidence that the place had changed with her. She went in silently, and the darkness was as day to her. Her own rooms were all shut up, yet were open to her steps, which no external obstacle could limit. There was still the sound of life below stairs, and in the housekeeper's room a cheerful party gathered round the fire. It was then that she turned first, with some wistful human attraction, towards the warmth and light rather than to the still places in which her own life had been passed. Mrs. Prentiss, the housekeeper, had her daughter with her on a visit, and the daughter's baby lay asleep in a cradle placed upon two chairs, outside the little circle of women round the table, one of whom was Jervis, Lady Mary's maid. Jervis sat and worked and cried, and mixed her words with little sobs. "I never thought as I should have had to take another place," she said. "Brown and me, we made sure of a little something to start upon. He's been here for twenty years, and so have you, Mrs. Prentiss; and me, as nobody can say I wasn't faithful night and day."

"I never had that confidence in my lady to expect anything," Prentiss said.

"Oh, mother, don't say that: many and many a day you've said, 'When my lady dies--'"

"And we've all said it," said Jervis. "I can't think how she did it, nor why she did it; for she was a kind lady, though appearances is against her."

"She was one of them, and I've known a many, as could not abide to see a gloomy face," said the housekeeper. "She kept us all comfortable for the sake of being comfortable herself, but no more."

"Oh, you are hard upon my lady!" cried Jervis, "and I can't bear to hear a word against her, though it's been an awful disappointment to me."

"What's you or me, or any one," cried Mrs. Prentiss, "in comparison of that poor little thing that can't work for her living like we can; that is left on the charity of folks she don't belong to? I'd have forgiven my lady anything, if she'd done what was right by Miss Mary. You'll get a place, and a good place; and me, they'll leave me here when the new folks come as have taken the house. But what will become of her, the darling? and not a penny, nor a friend, nor one to look to her? Oh, you selfish old woman! oh, you heart of stone! I just hope you are feeling it where you're gone," the housekeeper cried.

But as she said this, the woman did not know who was looking at her with wide, wistful eyes, holding out her hands in appeal, receiving every word as if it had been a blow,--though she knew it was useless. Lady Mary could not help it. She cried out to them, "Have pity upon me! Have pity upon me! I am not cruel, as you think," with a keen anguish in her voice, which seemed to be sharp enough to pierce the very air and go up to the skies. And so, perhaps, it did; but never touched the human atmosphere in which she stood a stranger. Jervis was threading her needle when her mistress uttered that cry; but her hand did not tremble, nor did the thread deflect a hair's-breadth from the straight line. The young mother alone seemed to be moved by some faint disturbance. "Hush!" she said, "is he waking?"--looking towards the cradle. But as the baby made no further sound, she too, returned to her sewing; and they sat bending their heads over their work round the table, and continued their talk. The room was very comfortable, bright, and warm, as Lady Mary had liked all her rooms to be. The warm firelight danced upon the walls; the women talked in cheerful tones. She stood outside their circle, and looked at them with a wistful face. Their notice would have been more sweet to her, as she stood in that great humiliation, than in other times the look of a queen.

"But what is the matter with baby?" the mother said, rising hastily.

It was with no servile intention of securing a look from that little prince of life that she who was not of this world had stepped aside forlorn, and looked at him in his cradle. Though she was not of this world, she was still a woman, and had nursed her children in her arms. She bent over the infant by the soft impulse of nature, tenderly, with no interested thought. But the child saw her; was it possible? He turned his head towards her, and flickered his baby hands, and cooed with that indescribable voice that goes to every woman's heart. Lady Mary felt such a thrill of pleasure go through her, as no incident had given her for long years. She put out her arms to him as his mother snatched him from his little bed; and he, which was more wonderful, stretched towards her in his innocence, turning away from them all.

"He wants to go to some one," cried the mother. "Oh look, look, for God's sake! Who is there that the child sees?"

"There's no one there,--not a soul. Now dearie, dearie, be reasonable. You can see for yourself there's not a creature," said the grandmother.

"Oh, my baby, my baby! He sees something we can't see," the young woman cried. "Something has happened to his father, or he's going to be taken from me!" she said, holding the child to her in a sudden passion. The other women rushed to her to console her,--the mother with reason, and Jervis with poetry. "It's the angels whispering, like the song says." Oh, the pang that was in the heart of the other whom they could not hear! She stood wondering how it could be,--wondering with an amazement beyond words, how all that was in her heart, the love and the pain, and the sweetness and bitterness, could all be hidden,--all hidden by that air in which the women stood so clear! She held out her hands, she spoke to them, telling who she was, but no one paid any attention; only the little dog Fido, who had been basking by the fire, sprang up, looked at her, and retreating slowly backwards till he reached the wall, sat down there and looked at her again, with now and then a little bark of inquiry. The dog saw her. This gave her a curious pang of humiliation, yet pleasure. She went away out of that little centre of human life in a great excitement and thrill of her whole being. The child had seen her, and the dog; but, oh heavens! how was she to work out her purpose by such auxiliaries as these?

She went up to her old bedchamber with unshed tears heavy about her eyes, and a pathetic smile quivering on her mouth. It touched her beyond measure that the child should have that confidence in her. "Then God is still with me," she said to herself. Her room, which had been so warm and bright, lay desolate in the still-ness of the night; but she wanted no light, for the darkness was no darkness to her. She looked round her for a little, wondering to think how far away from her now was this scene of her old life, but feeling no pain in the sight of it,--only a kind indulgence for the foolish simplicity which had taken so much pride in all these in-fantile elements of living. She went to the little Italian cabinet which stood against the wall, feeling now at least that she could do as she would,--that here there was no blank of human unconsciousness to stand in her way. But she was met by some-thing that baffled and vexed her once more. She felt the polished surface of the wood under her hand, and saw all the pretty ornamentation, the inlaid-work, the delicate carvings, which she knew so well; they swam in her eyes a little, as if they were part of some phantasmagoria about her, existing only in her vision. Yet the smooth surface resisted her touch; and when she withdrew a step from it, it stood before her solidly and square, as it had stood always--a glory to the place. She put forth her hands upon it, and could have traced the waving lines of the exquisite work, in which some artist soul had worked itself out in the old times; but though she thus saw it and felt, she could not with all her endeavors find the handle of the drawer, the richly-wrought knob of ivory, the little door that opened into the secret place. How long she stood by it, attempting again and again to find what was as familiar to her as her own hand, what was before her, visible in every line, what she felt with fingers which began to tremble, she could not tell. Time did not count with her as with common men. She did not grow weary, or require refreshment or rest, like those who were still of this world. Put at length her head grew giddy and her heart failed. A cold despair took possession of her soul. She could do nothing, then,--nothing; neither by help of man, neither by use of her own faculties, which were greater and clearer than ever before. She sank down upon the floor at the foot of that old toy, which had pleased her in the softness of her old age, to which she had trusted the fortunes of another; by which, in wantonness and folly she had sinned, she had sinned! And she thought she saw standing round her companions in the land she had left, saying, "It is impossible, impossible!" with infinite pity in their eyes; and the face of him who had given her permission to come, yet who had said no word to her to encourage her in what was against nature. And there came into her heart a longing to fly, to get home, to be back in the land where her fellows were, and her appointed place. A child lost, how pitiful that is! without power to reason and divine how help will come; but a soul lost, outside of one method of existence, withdrawn from the other, knowing no way to retrace its steps, nor how help can come! There had been no bitterness in passing from earth to the land where she had gone; but now there came upon her soul, in all the power of her new faculties, the bitterness of death. The place which was hers she had forsaken and left, and the place that had been hers knew her no more.

VII.

Mary, when she left her kind friend in the vicarage, went out and took a long walk. She had received a shock so great that it took all sensation from her, and threw her into the seething and surging of an excitement altogether beyond her control. She could not think until she had got familiar with the idea, which indeed had been vaguely shaping itself in her mind ever since she had emerged from the first profound gloom and prostration of the shadow of death. She had never definitely thought of her position before,--never even asked herself what was to become of her when Lady Mary died. She did not see, any more than Lady Mary did, why she should ever die; and girls, who have never wanted anything in their lives, who have had no sharp experience to enlighten them, are slow to think upon such subjects. She had not expected anything; her mind had not formed any idea of inheritance; and it had not surprised her to hear of the earl, who was Lady Mary's natural heir, nor to feel herself separated from the house in which all her previous life had been passed. But there had been gradually dawning upon her a sense that she had come to a crisis in her life, and that she must soon be told what was to become of her. It was not so urgent as that she should ask any questions; but it began to appear very clearly in her mind that things were not to be with her as they had been. She had heard the complaints and astonishment of the servants, to whom Lady Mary had left nothing, with resentment,--Jervis, who could not marry and take her lodging-house, but must wait until she had saved more money, and wept to think, after all her devotion, of having to take another place; and Mrs. Prentiss, the housekeeper, who was cynical, and expounded Lady Mary's kindness to her servants to be the issue of a refined selfishness; and Brown, who had sworn subdued oaths, and had taken the liberty of representing himself to Mary as "in the same box" with herself. Mary had been angry, very angry at all this;

and she had not by word or look given any one to understand that she felt herself "in the same box." But yet she had been vaguely anxious, curious, desiring to know. And she had not even begun to think what she should do. That seemed a sort of affront to her godmother's memory, at all events, until some one had made it clear to her. But now, in a moment, with her first consciousness of the importance of this matter in the sight of others, a consciousness of what it was to herself, came into her mind. A change of everything,--a new life,--a new world; and not only so, but a severance from the old world,--a giving up of everything that had been most near and pleasant to her.

These thoughts were driven through her mind like the snowflakes in a storm. The year had slid on since Lady Mary's death. Winter was beginning to yield to spring; the snow was over, and the great cold. And other changes had taken place. The great house had been let, and the family who had taken it had been about a week in possession. Their coming had inflicted a wound upon Mary's heart; but everybody had urged upon her the idea that it was much better the house should be let for a time, "till everything was settled." When all was settled, things would be different. Mrs. Vicar did not say, "You can then do what you please," but she did convey to Mary's mind somehow a sort of inference that she would have something to do it with. And when Mary had protested. "It shall never be let again with my will," the kind woman had said tremulously, "Well, my dear!" and had changed the subject. All these things now came to Mary's mind. They had been afraid to tell her; they had thought it would be so much to her,--so important, such a crushing blow. To have nothing,--to be destitute; to be written about by Mr. Furnival to the earl; to have her case represented,--Mary felt herself stung by such unendurable suggestions into an energy--a determination--of which her soft young life had known nothing. No one should write about her, or ask charity for her, she said to herself. She had gone through the woods and round the park, which was not large, and now she could not leave these beloved precincts without going to look at the house. Up to this time she had not had the courage to go near the house; but to the commotion and fever of her mind every violent sensation was congenial, and she went up the avenue now almost gladly, with a little demonstration to herself of energy and courage. Why not that as well as all the rest?

It was once more twilight, and the dimness favored her design. She wanted to go there unseen, to look up at the windows with their alien lights, and to think of the time when Lady Mary sat behind the curtains, and there was nothing but tenderness and peace throughout the house. There was a light in every window along the entire front, a lavishness of firelight and lamplight which told of a household in which there were many inhabitants. Mary's mind was so deeply absorbed, and perhaps her eyes so dim with tears that she could scarcely see what was before her, when the door opened suddenly and a lady came out. "I will go myself," she said in an agitated tone to some one behind her. "Don't get yourself laughed at," said a voice from within. The sound of the voices roused the young spectator. She looked with a little curiosity, mixed with anxiety, at the lady who had come out of the house, and who started, too, with a gesture of alarm, when she saw Mary move in the dark. "Who are you?" she cried out in a trembling voice, "and what do you want here?"

Then Mary made a step or two forward and said, "I must ask your pardon if I am trespassing. I did not know there was any objection--" This stranger to make an objection! It brought something like a tremulous laugh to Mary's lips.

"Oh, there is no objection," said the lady, "only we have been a little put out. I see now; you are the young lady who--you are the young lady that--you are the one that--suffered most."

"I am Lady Mary's goddaughter," said the girl. "I have lived here all my life."

"Oh, my dear, I have heard all about you," the lady cried. The people who had taken the house were merely rich people; they had no other characteristic; and in the vicarage, as well as in the other houses about, it was said, when they were spoken of, that it was a good thing they were not people to be visited, since nobody could have had the heart to visit strangers in Lady Mary's house. And Mary could not but feel a keen resentment to think that her story, such as it was, the story which she had only now heard in her own person, should be discussed by such people. But the speaker had a look of kindness, and, so far as could be seen, of perplexity and fretted anxiety in her face, and had been in a hurry, but stopped herself in order to show her interest. "I wonder," she said impulsively, "that you can come here and look at the place again, after all that has passed."

"I never thought," said Mary, "that there could be--any objection."

"Oh, how can you think I mean that?--how can you pretend to think so?" cried the other, impatiently. "But after you have been treated so heartlessly, so unkindly,--and left, poor thing! they tell me, without a penny, without any provision--"

"I don't know you," cried Mary, breathless with quick rising passion. "I don't know what right you can have to meddle with my affairs."

The lady stared at her for a moment without speaking, and then she said, all at once, "That is quite true,--but it is rude as well; for though I have no right to meddle with your affairs, I did it in kindness, because I took an interest in you from all I have heard."

Mary was very accessible to such a reproach and argument. Her face flushed with a sense of her own churlishness. "I beg your pardon," she said; "I am sure you mean to be kind."

"Well," said the stranger, "that is perhaps going too far on the other side, for you can't even see my face, to know what I mean. But I do mean to be kind, and I am very sorry for you. And though I think you've been treated abominably, all the same I like you better for not allowing any one to say so. And now, do you know where I was going? I was going to the vicarage,--where you are living, I believe,--to see if the vicar, or his wife, or you, or all of you together, could do a thing for me."

"Oh, I am sure Mrs. Bowyer--" said Mary, with a voice much less assured than her words.

"You must not be too sure, my dear. I know she doesn't mean to call upon me, because my husband is a city man. That is just as she pleases. I am not very fond of city men myself. But there's no reason why I should stand on ceremony when I want something, is there? Now, my dear, I want to know--Don't laugh at me. I am not superstitious, so far as I am aware; but--Tell me, in your time was there ever any disturbance, any appearance you couldn't understand, any--Well, I don't like the word ghost. It's disrespectful, if there's anything of the sort: and it's vulgar if there isn't. But you know what I mean. Was there anything--of that sort--in your time?"

In your time! Poor Mary had scarcely realized yet that her time was over. Her heart refused to allow it when it was thus so abruptly brought before her, but she obliged herself to subdue these rising rebellions, and to answer, though with some *hauteur*, "There is nothing of the kind that I ever heard of. There is no superstition or ghost in our house."

She thought it was the vulgar desire of new people to find a conventional mystery, and it seemed to Mary that this was a desecration of her home. Mrs. Turner, however (for that was her name), did not receive the intimation as the girl expected, but looked at her very gravely, and said, "That makes it a great deal more serious," as if to herself. She paused and then added, "You see, the case is this. I have a little girl who is our youngest, who is just my husband's idol. She is a sweet little thing, though perhaps I should not say it. Are you fond of children? Then I almost feel sure you would think so too. Not a moping child at all, or too clever, or anything to alarm one. Well, you know, little Connie, since ever we came in, has seen an old lady walking about the house."

"An old lady!" said Mary, with an involuntary smile.

"Oh, yes. I laughed too, the first time. I said it would be old Mrs. Prentiss, or perhaps the char-woman, or some old lady from the village that had been in the habit of coming in the former people's time. But the child got very angry. She said it was a real lady. She would not allow me to speak. Then we thought perhaps it was some one who did not know the house was let, and had walked in to look at it; but nobody would go on coming like that with all the signs of a large family in the house. And now the doctor says the child must be low, that the place perhaps doesn't agree with her, and that we must send her away. Now I ask you, how could I send little Connie away, the apple of her father's eye? I should have to go with her, of course, and how could the house get on without me? Naturally we are very anxious. And this afternoon she has seen her again, and sits there crying because she says the dear old lady looks so sad. I just seized my hat, and walked out, to come to you and your friends at the vicarage, to see if you could help me. Mrs. Bowyer may look down upon a city person,--I don't mind that; but she is a mother, and surely she would feel for a mother," cried the poor lady vehemently, putting up her hands to her wet eyes.

"Oh, indeed, indeed she would! I am sure now that she will call directly. We did not know what a--" Mary stopped herself in saying, "what a nice woman you are," which she thought would be rude, though poor Mrs. Turner would have liked it. But then she shook her head and added, "What could any of us do to help you? I have never heard of any old lady. There never was anything--I know all about the house, everything that has ever happened, and Prentiss will tell you. There is nothing of that kind,--indeed, there is nothing. You must have--" But here Mary stopped again; for to suggest that a new family, a city family, should have brought an apparition of their own with them, was too ridiculous an idea to be entertained.

"Miss Vivian," said Mrs. Turner, "will you come back with me and speak to the child?"

At this Mary faltered a little. "I have never been there--since the--funeral," she said.

The good woman laid a kind hand upon her shoulder, caressing and soothing. "You were very fond of her--in spite of the way she has used you?"

"Oh, how dare you, or any one, to speak of her so! She used me as if I had been her dearest child. She was more kind to me than a mother. There is no one in the world like her!" Mary cried.

"And yet she left you without a penny. Oh, you must be a good girl to feel for her like that. She left you without--What are you going to do, my dear? I feel like a friend. I feel like a mother to you, though you don't know me. You mustn't think it is only curiosity. You can't stay with your friends for ever,--and what are you going to do?"

There are some cases in which it is more easy to speak to a stranger than to one's dearest and oldest friend. Mary had felt this when she rushed out, not knowing how to tell the vicar's wife that she must leave her, and find some independence for herself. It was, however, strange to rush into such a discussion with so little warning, and Mary's pride was very sensitive. She said, "I am not going to burden my friends," with a little indignation; but then she remembered how forlorn she was, and her voice softened. "I must do something,--but I don't know what I am good for," she said, trembling, and on the verge of tears.

"My dear, I have heard a great deal about you," said the stranger; "it is not rash, though it may look so. Come back with me directly, and see Connie. She is a very interesting little thing, though I say it; it is wonderful sometimes to hear her talk. You shall be her governess, my dear. Oh, you need not teach her anything,--that is not what I mean. I think, I am sure, you will be the saving of her, Miss Vivian; and such a lady as you are, it will be everything for the other girls to live with you. Don't stop to think, but just come with me. You shall have whatever you please, and always be treated like a lady. Oh, my dear, consider my feelings as a mother, and come; oh, come to Connie! I know you will save her; it is an inspiration. Come back! Come back with me!"

It seemed to Mary too like an inspiration. What it cost her to cross that threshold and walk in a stranger, to the house which had been all her life as her own, she never said to any one. But it was independence; it was deliverance from entreaties and remonstrances without end. It was a kind of setting right, so far as could be, of the balance which had got so terribly wrong. No writing to the earl now; no appeal to friends; anything in all the world,--much more, honest service and kindness,--must be better than that.

VIII.

Tell the young lady all about it, Connie," said her mother.

But Connie was very reluctant to tell. She was very shy, and clung to her mother, and hid her face in her ample dress; and though presently she was beguiled by Mary's voice, and in a short time came to her side, and clung to her as she had clung to Mrs. Turner, she still kept her secret to herself. They were all very kind to Mary, the elder girls standing round in a respectful circle looking at her, while their mother exhorted them to "take a pattern" by Miss Vivian. The novelty, the awe which she inspired, the real kindness about her, ended in overcoming in Mary's young mind the first miserable impression of such a return to her home. It gave her a kind of pleasure to write to Mrs. Bowyer that she had found employment, and had thought it better to accept it at once. "Don't be angry with me; and I think you will understand me," she said. And then she gave herself up to the strange new scene.

The "ways" of the large simple-minded family, homely, yet kindly, so transformed Lady Mary's graceful old rooms that they no longer looked the same place. And when Mary sat down with them at the big heavy-laden table, surrounded with the hum of so large a party, it was impossible for her to believe that everything was not new about her. In no way could the saddening recollections of a home from which the chief figure had disappeared, have been more completely broken up. Afterwards Mrs. Turner took her aside, and begged to know which was Mary's old room, "for I should like to put you there, as if nothing had happened." "Oh, do not put me there!" Mary cried, "so much has happened." But this seemed a refinement to the kind woman, which it was far better for her young guest not to "yield" to. The room Mary had occupied had been next to her godmother's, with a door between, and when it turned out that Connie, with an elder sister, was in Lady Mary's

room, everything seemed perfectly arranged in Mrs. Turner's eyes. She thought
it was providential,--with a simple belief in Mary's powers that in other circumstances would have been amusing. But there was no amusement in Mary's mind
when she took possession of the old room "as if nothing had happened." She sat by
the fire for half the night, in an agony of silent recollection and thought, going over
the last days of her godmother's life, calling up everything before her, and realizing
as she had never realized till now, the lonely career on which she was setting out,
the subjection to the will and convenience of strangers in which henceforth her life
must be passed. This was a kind woman who had opened her doors to the destitute
girl; but notwithstanding, however great the torture to Mary, there was no escap-
ing this room which was haunted by the saddest recollections of her life. Of such
things she must no longer complain,--nay, she must think of nothing but thanking
the mistress of the house for her thoughtfulness, for the wish to be kind, which so
often exceeds the performance.

The room was warm and well lighted; the night was very calm and sweet outside, nothing had been touched or changed of all her little decorations, the ornaments which had been so delightful to her girlhood. A large photograph of Lady
Mary held the chief place over the mantel-piece, representing her in the fullness
of her beauty,--a photograph which had been taken from the picture painted ages
ago by a Royal Academician. It fortunately was so little like Lady Mary in her old
age that, save as a thing which had always hung there, and belonged to her happier
life, it did not affect the girl; but no picture was necessary to bring before her the
well-remembered figure. She could not realize that the little movements she heard
on the other side of the door were any other than those of her mistress, her friend,
her mother; for all these names Mary lavished upon her in the fullness of her heart.
The blame that was being cast upon Lady Mary from all sides made this child of her
bounty but more deeply her partisan, more warm in her adoration. She would not,
for all the inheritances of the world, have acknowledged even to herself that Lady
Mary was in fault. Mary felt that she would rather a thousand times be poor and
have to gain her daily bread, than that she who had nourished and cherished her
should have been forced in her cheerful old age to think, before she chose to do so,
of parting and farewell and the inevitable end.

She thought, like every young creature in strange and painful circumstances, that she would be unable to sleep, and did indeed lie awake and weep for an hour or more, thinking of all the changes that had happened; but sleep overtook her before she knew, while her mind was still full of these thoughts; and her dreams were endless, confused, full of misery and longing. She dreamed a dozen times over that she heard Lady Mary's soft call through the open door,--which was not open, but shut closely and locked by the sisters who now inhabited the next room; and once she dreamed that Lady Mary came to her bedside and stood there looking at her earnestly, with the tears flowing from her eyes. Mary struggled in her sleep to tell her benefactress how she loved her, and approved of all she had done, and wanted nothing,--but felt herself bound as by a nightmare, so that she could not move or speak, or even put out a hand to dry those tears which it was intolerable to her to see; and woke with the struggle, and the miserable sensation of seeing her dearest friend weep and being unable to comfort her. The moon was shining into the room, throwing part of it into a cold, full light, while blackness lay in all corners. The impression of her dream was so strong that Mary's eyes turned instantly to the spot where in her dream her godmother had stood. To be sure, there was nobody there; but as her consciousness returned, and with it the sweep of painful recollection, the sense of change, the miserable contrast between the present and the past,--sleep fled from her eyes. She fell into the vividly awake condition which is the alternative of broken sleep, and gradually, as she lay, there came upon her that mysterious sense of another presence in the room which is so subtle and indescribable. She neither saw anything nor heard anything, and yet she felt that some one was there.

She lay still for some time and held her breath, listening for a movement, even for the sound of breathing,--scarcely alarmed, yet sure that she was not alone. After a while she raised herself on her pillow, and in a low voice asked, "Who is there? is any one there?" There was no reply, no sound of any description, and yet the conviction grew upon her. Her heart began to beat, and the blood to mount to her head. Her own being made so much sound, so much commotion, that it seemed to her she could not hear anything save those beatings and pulsings. Yet she was not afraid. After a time, however, the oppression became more than she could bear. She got up and lit her candle, and searched through the familiar room; but she found no trace that any one had been there. The furniture was all in its usual order. There was no hiding-place where any human thing could find refuge. When she had satisfied herself, and was about to return to bed, suppressing a sensation which must, she said to herself, be altogether fantastic, she was startled by a low knocking at the door of communication. Then she heard the voice of the elder girl. "Oh, Miss Vivian what is it? Have you seen anything?" A new sense of anger, disdain, humiliation, swept through Mary's mind. And if she had seen anything, she said to herself, what was that to those strangers? She replied, "No, nothing; what should I see?" in a tone which was almost haughty, in spite of herself.

"I thought it might be--the ghost. Oh, please, don't be angry. I thought I heard this door open, but it is locked. Oh! perhaps it is very silly, but I am so frightened, Miss Vivian."

"Go back to bed," said Mary; "there is no--ghost. I am going to sit up and write some--letters. You will see my light under the door."

"Oh, thank you," cried the girl.

Mary remembered what a consolation and strength in all wakefulness had been the glimmer of the light under her godmother's door. She smiled to think that she herself, so desolate as she was, was able to afford this innocent comfort to another girl, and then sat down and wept quietly, feeling her solitude and the chill about her, and the dark and the silence. The moon had gone behind a cloud. There seemed no light but her small miserable candle in earth and heaven. And yet that poor little speck of light kept up the heart of another,--which made her smile again in the middle of her tears. And by-and-by the commotion in her head and heart calmed down, and she too fell asleep.

Next day she heard all the floating legends that were beginning to rise in the house. They all arose from Connie's questions about the old lady whom she had seen going up-stairs before her, the first evening after the new family's arrival. It was in the presence of the doctor,--who had come to see the child, and whose surprise at finding Mary there was almost ludicrous,--that she heard the story, though much against his will.

"There can be no need for troubling Miss Vivian about it," he said, in a tone which was almost rude. But Mrs. Turner was not sensitive.

"When Miss Vivian has just come like a dear, to help us with Connie!" the good woman cried. "Of course she must hear it, doctor, for otherwise, how could she know what to do?"

"Is it true that you have come here--here? to help--Good heavens, Miss Mary, *here?*"

"Why not here?" Mary said, smiling as but she could. "I am Connie's governess, doctor."

He burst out into that suppressed roar which serves a man instead of tears, and jumped up from his seat, clenching his fist. The clenched fist was to the intention of the dead woman whose fault this was; and if it had ever entered the doctor's mind, as his mother supposed, to marry this forlorn child, and thus bestow a home upon her whether she would or no, no doubt he would now have attempted to carry out that plan. But as no such thing had occurred to him, the doctor only showed his sense of the intolerable by look and gesture. "I must speak to the vicar. I must see Furnival. It can't be permitted," he cried.

"Do you think I shall not be kind to her, doctor?" cried Mrs. Turner. "Oh, ask her! she is one that understands. She knows far better than that. We're not fine people, doctor, but we're kind people. I can say that for myself. There is nobody in this house but will be good to her, and admire her, and take an example by her. To have a real lady with the girls, that is what I would give anything for; and as she wants taking care of, poor dear, and petting, and an 'ome--" Mary, who would not hear any more, got up hastily, and took the hand of her new protectress, and kissed her, partly out of gratitude and kindness, partly to stop her mouth, and prevent the saying of something which it might have been still more difficult to support. "You are a real lady yourself, dear Mrs. Turner," she cried. (And this notwithstanding the one deficient letter: but many people who are much more dignified than Mrs. Turner-- people who behave themselves very well in every other respect--say "'ome.")

"Oh, my dear, I don't make any pretensions," the good woman cried, but with a little shock of pleasure which brought the tears to her eyes.

And then the story was told. Connie had seen the lady walk up-stairs, and had thought no harm. The child supposed it was some one belonging to the house. She had gone into the room which was now Connie's room; but as that had a second door, there was no suspicion caused by the fact that she was not found there a little time after, when the child told her mother what she had seen. After this, Connie had seen the same lady several times, and once had met her face to face. The child declared that she was not at all afraid. She was a pretty old lady, with white hair and dark eyes. She looked a little sad, but smiled when Connie stopped and stared at her,--not angry at all, but rather pleased,--and looked for a moment as if she would speak. That was all. Not a word about a ghost was said in Connie's hearing. She had already told it all to the doctor, and he had pretended to consider which of the old ladies in the neighborhood this could be. In Mary's mind, occupied as it was by so many important matters, there had been up to this time no great question about Connie's apparition; now she began to listen closely, not so much from real interest as from a perception that the doctor, who was her friend, did not want her to hear. This naturally aroused her attention at once. She listened to the child's description with growing eagerness, all the more because the doctor opposed. "Now that will do, Miss Connie," he said; "it is one of the old Miss Murchisons, who are always so fond of finding out about their neighbors. I have no doubt at all on that subject. She wants to find you out in your pet naughtiness, whatever it is, and tell me."

"I am sure it is not for that," cried Connie. "Oh, how can you be so disagreeable? I know she is not a lady who would tell. Besides, she is not thinking at all about me. She was either looking for something she had lost, or,--oh, I don't know what it was!--and when she saw me she just smiled. She is not dressed like any of the people here. She had got no cloak on, or bonnet, or anything that is common, but a beautiful white shawl and a long dress, and it gives a little sweep when she walks,--oh no! not like your rustling, mamma; but all soft, like water,--and it looks like lace upon her head, tied here," said Connie, putting her hands to her chin, "in such a pretty, large, soft knot." Mary had gradually risen as this description went on, starting a little at first, looking up, getting upon her feet. The color went altogether out of her face,--her eyes grew to twice their natural size. The doctor put out his hand without looking at her, and laid it on her arm with a strong, emphatic pressure. "Just like some one you have seen a picture of," he said.

"Oh no. I never saw a picture that was so pretty," said the child.

"Doctor, why do you ask her any more? don't you see, don't you see, the child has seen--"

"Miss Mary, for God's sake, hold your tongue; it is folly, you know. Now, my little girl, tell me. I know this old lady is the very image of that pretty old lady with the toys for good children, who was in the last Christmas number?"

"Oh!" said Connie, pausing a little. "Yes, I remember; it was a very pretty picture,--mamma put it up in the nursery. No, she is not like that, not at all, much prettier; and then *my* lady is sorry about something,--except when she smiles at me. She has her hair put up like this, and this," the child went on, twisting her own bright locks.

"Doctor, I can't bear any more."

"My dear, you are mistaken, it is all a delusion. She has seen a picture. I think now, Mrs. Turner, that my little patient had better run away and play. Take a good run through the woods, Miss Connie, with your brother, and I will send you some physic which will not be at all nasty, and we shall hear no more of your old lady. My dear Miss Vivian, if you will but hear reason! I have known such cases a hundred times. The child has seen a picture, and it has taken possession of her imagination. She is a little below par, and she has a lively imagination; and she has learned something from Prentiss, though probably she does not remember that. And there it is! a few doses of quinine, and she will see visions no more."

"Doctor," cried Mary, "how can you speak so to me? You dare not look me in the face. You know you dare not: as if you did not know as well as I do! Oh, why does that child see her, and not me?"

"There it is," he said, with a broken laugh. "Could anything show better that it is a mere delusion? Why, in the name of all that is reasonable, should this stranger child see her, if it was anything, and not you?"

Mrs. Turner looked from one to another with wondering eyes. "You know what it is?" she said. "Oh, you know what it is? Doctor, doctor, is it because my Connie is so delicate? Is it a warning? Is it--"

"Oh, for heaven's sake! You will drive me mad, you ladies. Is it this, and is it that? It is nothing, I tell you. The child is out of sorts, and she has seen some picture that has caught her fancy,--and she thinks she sees--I'll send her a bottle," he cried, jumping up, "that will put an end to all that."

"Doctor, don't go away, tell me rather what I must do--if she is looking for something! Oh, doctor, think if she were unhappy, if she were kept out of her sweet rest!"

"Miss Mary, for God's sake, be reasonable. You ought never to have heard a word."

"Doctor, think! if it should be anything we can do. Oh, tell me, tell me! Don't go away and leave me; perhaps we can find out what it is."

"I will have nothing to do with your findings out. It is mere delusion. Put them both to bed, Mrs. Turner; put them all to bed!--as if there was not trouble enough!"

"What is it?" cried Connie's mother; "is it a warning! Oh, for the love of God, tell me, is that what comes before a death?"

When they were all in this state of agitation, the vicar and his wife were suddenly shown into the room. Mrs. Bowyer's eyes flew to Mary, but she was too well bred a woman not to pay her respects first to the lady of the house, and there were a number of politenesses exchanged, very breathlessly on Mrs. Turner's part, before the new-comers were free to show the real occasion of their visit. "Oh, Mary, what did you mean by taking such a step all in a moment? How could you come here, of all places in the world? And how could you leave me without a word?" the vicar's wife said, with her lips against Mary's cheek. She had already perceived, without dwelling upon it, the excitement in which all the party were. This was said while the vicar was still making his bow to his new parishioner, who knew very well that her visitors had not intended to call; for the Turners were dissenters, to crown all their misdemeanors, beside being city people and *nouveaux riches*.

"Don't ask me any questions just now," said Mary, clasping almost hysterically her friend's hand.

"It was providential. Come and hear what the child has seen." Mrs. Turner, though she was so anxious, was too polite not to make a fuss about getting chairs for all her visitors. She postponed her own trouble to this necessity, and trembling, sought the most comfortable seat for Mrs. Bowyer, the largest and most imposing for the vicar himself. When she had established them in a little circle, and done her best to draw Mary, too, into a chair, she sat down quietly, her mind divided between the cares of courtesy and the alarms of an anxious mother. Mary stood at the table and waited till the commotion was over. The new-comers thought she was going to explain her conduct in leaving them; and Mrs. Bowyer, at least, who was critical in point of manners, shivered a little, wondering if perhaps (though she could not find it in her heart to blame Mary) her proceedings were in perfect taste.

"The little girl," Mary said, beginning abruptly. She had been standing by the table, her lips apart, her countenance utterly pale, her mind evidently too much absorbed to notice anything. "The little girl has seen several times a lady going up-stairs. Once she met her and saw her face, and the lady smiled at her; but her face was sorrowful, and the child thought she was looking for something. The lady was old, with white hair done up upon her forehead, and lace upon her head. She was dressed--" here Mary's voice began to be interrupted from time to time by a brief sob--"in a long dress that made a soft sound when she walked, and a white shawl, and the lace tied under her chin in a large soft knot--"

"Mary, Mary!" Mrs. Bowyer had risen and stood behind the girl, in whose slender throat the climbing sorrow was almost visible, supporting her, trying to stop her. "Mary, Mary!" she cried; "oh, my darling, what are you thinking of? Francis! doctor! make her stop, make her stop."

"Why should she stop?" said Mrs. Turner, rising, too, in her agitation. "Oh, is it a warning, is it a warning? for my child has seen it,--Connie has seen it."

"Listen to me, all of you," said Mary, with an effort. "You all know--who that is. And she has seen her,--the little girl--"

Now the others looked at each other, exchanging a startled look.

"My dear people," cried the doctor, "the case is not the least unusual. No, no, Mrs. Turner, it is no warning,--it is nothing of the sort. Look here, Bowyer; you'll believe me. The child is very nervous and sensitive. She has evidently seen a picture somewhere of our dear old friend. She has heard the story somehow,--oh, perhaps in some garbled version from Prentiss, or--of course they've all been talking of it. And the child is one of those creatures with its nerves all on the surface,--and a little below par in health, in need of iron and quinine, and all that sort of thing. I've seen a hundred such cases," cried the doctor, "--a thousand such; but now, of course, we'll have a fine story made of it, now that it's come into the ladies' hands."

He was much excited with this long speech; but it cannot be said that any one paid much attention to him. Mrs. Bowyer was holding Mary in her arms, uttering little cries and sobs over her, and looking anxiously at her husband. The vicar sat down suddenly in his chair, with the air of a man who has judgment to deliver without the least idea what to say; while Mary, freeing herself unconsciously from her friend's restraining embrace, stood facing them all with a sort of trembling defiance; and Mrs. Turner kept on explaining nervously that,--"no, no, her Connie was not excitable, was not oversensitive, had never known what a delusion was."

"This is very strange," the vicar said.

"Oh, Mr. Bowyer," cried Mary, "tell me what I am to do!--think if she cannot rest, if she is not happy, she that was so good to everybody, that never could bear to see any one in trouble. Oh, tell me, tell me what I am to do! It is you that have disturbed her with all you have been saying. Oh, what can I do, what can I do to give her rest?"

"My dear Mary! my dear Mary!" they all cried, in different tones of consternation; and for a few minutes no one could speak. Mrs. Bowyer, as was natural, said something, being unable to endure the silence; but neither she nor any of the others knew what it was she said. When it was evident that the vicar must speak, all were silent, waiting for him; and though it now became imperative that something in the shape of a judgment must be delivered, yet he was as far as ever from knowing what to say.

"Mary," he said, with a little tremulousness of voice, "it is quite natural that you should ask me; but, my dear, I am not at all prepared to answer. I think you know that the doctor, who ought to know best about such matters--"

"Nay, not I. I only know about the physical; the other,--if there is another,-- that's your concern."

"Who ought to know best," repeated Mr. Bowyer; "for every body will tell you, my dear, that the mind is so dependent upon the body. I suppose he must be right. I suppose it is just the imagination of a nervous child working upon the data which have been given,--the picture; and then, as you justly remind me, all we have been saying--"

"How could the child know what we have been saying, Francis?"

"Connie has heard nothing that any one has been saying; and there is no picture."

"My dear lady, you hear what the doctor says. If there is no picture, and she has heard nothing, I suppose, then, your premises are gone, and the conclusion falls to the ground."

"What does it matter about premises?" cried the vicar's wife; "here is something dreadful that has happened. Oh, what nonsense that is about imagination; children have no imagination. A dreadful thing has happened. In heaven's name, Francis, tell this poor child what she is to do."

"My dear," said the vicar again, "you are asking me to believe in purgatory,--nothing less. You are asking me to contradict the church's teaching. Mary, you must compose yourself. You must wait till this excitement has passed away."

"I can see by her eyes that she did not sleep last night," the doctor said, relieved. "We shall have her seeing visions too, if we don't take care."

"And, my dear Mary," said the vicar, "if you will think of it, it is derogatory to the dignity of--of our dear friends who have passed away. How can we suppose that one of the blessed would come down from heaven, and walk about her own house, which she had just left, and show herself to a--to a--little child who had never seen her before."

"Impossible," said the doctor. "I told you so; a stranger--that had no connection with her, knew nothing about her--"

"Instead of," said the vicar, with a slight tremor, "making herself known, if that was permitted, to--to me, for example, or our friend here."

"That sounds reasonable, Mary," said Mrs. Bowyer; "don't you think so, my dear? If she had come to one of us, or to yourself, my darling, I should never have wondered, after all that has happened. But to this little child--"

"Whereas there is nothing more likely--more consonant with all the teachings of science--than that the little thing should have this hallucination, of which you ought never to have heard a word. You are the very last person--"

"That is true," said the vicar, "and all the associations of the place must be over-whelming. My dear, we must take her away with us. Mrs. Turner, I am sure, is very kind, but it cannot be good for Mary to be here."

"No, no! I never thought so," said Mrs. Bowyer. "I never intended--dear Mrs. Turner, we all appreciate your motives. I hope you will let us see much of you, and that we may become very good friends. But Mary--it is her first grief, don't you know?" said the vicar's wife, with the tears in her eyes; "she has always been so much cared for, so much thought of all her life--and then all at once! You will not think that we misunderstand your kind motives; but it is more than she can bear. She made up her mind in a hurry, without thinking. You must not be annoyed if we take her away."

Mrs. Turner had been looking from one to another while this dialogue went on. She said now, a little wounded, "I wished only to do what was kind; but, perhaps I was thinking most of my own child. Miss Vivian must do what she thinks best."

"You are all kind--too kind," Mary cried; "but no one must say another word, please. Unless Mrs. Turner should send me away, until I know what this all means, it is my place to stay here."

IX.

It was Lady Mary who had come into the vicarage that afternoon when Mrs. Bowyer supposed some one had called. She wandered about to a great many places in these days, but always returned to the scenes in which her life had been passed, and where alone her work could be done, if it could be done at all. She came in and listened while the tale of her own carelessness and heedlessness was told, and stood by while her favorite was taken to another woman's bosom for comfort, and heard everything and saw everything. She was used to it by this time; but to be nothing is hard, even when you are accustomed to it; and though she knew that they would not hear her, what could she do but cry out to them as she stood there unregarded? "Oh, have pity upon me!" Lady Mary said; and the pang in her heart was so great that the very atmosphere was stirred, and the air could scarcely contain her and the passion of her endeavor to make herself known, but thrilled like a harp-string to her cry. Mrs. Bowyer heard the jar and tingle in the inanimate world, but she thought only that it was some charitable visitor who had come in, and gone softly away again at the sound of tears.

And if Lady Mary could not make herself known to the poor cottagers who had loved her, or to the women who wept for her loss while they blamed her, how was she to reveal herself and her secret to the men who, if they had seen her, would have thought her an hallucination? Yes, she tried all, and even went a long journey over land and sea to visit the earl, who was her heir, and awake in him an interest in her child. And she lingered about all these people in the silence of the night, and tried to move them in dreams, since she could not move them waking. It is more easy for one who is no more of this world, to be seen and heard in sleep; for then those who are still in the flesh stand on the borders of the unseen, and see and hear things which, waking, they do not understand. But, alas! when they woke, this poor wanderer discovered that her friends remembered no more what she had said to them in their dreams.

Presently, however, when she found Mary established in her old home, in her old room, there came to her a new hope. For there is nothing in the world so hard to believe, or to be convinced of, as that no effort, no device, will ever make you known and visible to those you love. Lady Mary being little altered in her character, though so much in her being, still believed that if she could but find the way, in a moment,--in the twinkling of an eye, all would be revealed and understood. She went to Mary's room with this new hope strong in her heart. When they were alone together in that nest of comfort which she had herself made beautiful for her child,--two hearts so full of thought for each other,--what was there in earthly bonds which could prevent them from meeting? She went into the silent room, which was so familiar and dear, and waited like a mother long separated from her child, with a faint doubt trembling on the surface of her mind, yet a quaint, joyful confidence underneath in the force of nature. A few words would be enough,--a moment, and all would be right. And then she pleased herself with fancies of how, when that was done, she would whisper to her darling what has never been told to flesh and blood; and so go home proud, and satisfied, and happy in the accomplishment of all she had hoped.

Mary came in with her candle in her hand, and closed the door between her and all external things. She looked round wistful with that strange consciousness which she had already experienced, that some one was there. The other stood so close to her that the girl could not move without touching her. She held up her hands, imploring, to the child of her love. She called to her, "Mary, Mary!" putting her hands upon her, and gazed into her face with an intensity and anguish of eagerness which might have drawn the stars out of the sky. And a strange tumult was in Mary's bosom. She stood looking blankly round her, like one who is blind with open eyes, and saw nothing; and strained her ears like a deaf man, but heard nothing. All was silence, vacancy, an empty world about her. She sat down at her little table, with a heavy sigh. "The child can see her, but she will not come to me," Mary said, and wept.

Then Lady Mary turned away with a heart full of despair. She went quickly from the house, out into the night. The pang of her disappointment was so keen, that she could not endure it. She remembered what had been said to her in the place from whence she came, and how she had been entreated to be patient and wait. Oh, had she but waited and been patient! She sat down upon the ground, a soul forlorn, outside of life, outside of all things, lost in a world which had no place for her. The moon shone, but she made no shadow in it; the rain fell upon her, but did not hurt her; the little night breeze blew without finding any resistance in her. She said to herself, "I have failed. What am I, that I should do what they all said was impossible? It was my pride, because I have had my own way all my life. But now I have no way and no place on earth, and what I have to tell them will never, never be known. Oh, my little Mary, a servant in her own house! And a word would make it right!--but never, never can she hear that word. I am wrong to say never; she will know when she is in heaven. She will not live to be old and foolish, like me. She will go up there early, and then she will know. But I, what will become of me?--for I am nothing here, I cannot go back to my own place."

A little moaning wind rose up suddenly in the middle of the dark night, and carried a faint wail, like the voice of some one lost, to the windows of the great house. It woke the children and Mary, who opened her eyes quickly in the dark, wondering if perhaps now the vision might come to her. But the vision had come when she could not see it, and now returned no more.

X.

On the other side, however, visions which had nothing sacred in them began to be heard of, and "Connie's ghost," as it was called in the house, had various vulgar effects. A housemaid became hysterical, and announced that she too had seen the lady, of whom she gave a description, exaggerated from Connie's, which all the household were ready to swear she had never heard. The lady, whom Connie had only seen passing, went to Betsey's room in the middle of the night, and told her, in a hollow and terrible voice, that she could not rest, opening a series of communications by which it was evident all the secrets of the unseen world would soon be disclosed. And following upon this, there came a sort of panic in the house; noises were heard in various places, sounds of footsteps pacing, and of a long robe sweeping about the passages; and Lady Mary's costumes, and the head-dress which was so peculiar, which all her friends had recognized in Connie's description, grew into something portentous under the heavier hand of the foot-boy and the kitchen-maid. Mrs. Prentiss, who had remained, as a special favor to the new people, was deeply indignant and outraged by this treatment of her mistress. She appealed to Mary with mingled anger and tears.

"I would have sent the hussy away at an hour's notice, if I had the power in my hands," she cried, "but, Miss Mary, it's easily seen who is a real lady and who is not. Mrs. Turner interferes herself in everything, though she likes it to be supposed that she has a housekeeper."

"Dear Prentiss, you must not say Mrs. Turner is not a lady. She has far more delicacy of feeling than many ladies," cried Mary.

"Yes, Miss Mary, dear, I allow that she is very nice to you; but who could help that? and to hear my lady's name--that might have her faults, but who was far above anything of the sort--in every mouth, and her costume, that they don't know how to describe, and to think that *she* would go and talk to the like of Betsy Barnes about what is on her mind! I think sometimes I shall break my, heart, or else throw up my place, Miss Mary," Prentiss said, with tears.

"Oh, don't do that; oh, don't leave me, Prentiss!" Mary said, with an involuntary cry of dismay.

"Not if you mind, not if you mind, dear," the housekeeper cried. And then she drew close to the young lady with an anxious look. "You haven't seen anything?" she said. "That would be only natural, Miss Mary. I could well understand she couldn't rest in her grave,--if she came and told it all to you."

"Prentiss, be silent," cried Mary; "that ends everything between you and me, if you say such a word. There has been too much said already,--oh, far too much! as if I only loved her for what she was to leave me."

"I did not mean that, dear," said Prentiss; "but--"

"There is no but; and everything she did was right," the girl cried with vehemence. She shed hot and bitter tears over this wrong which all her friends did to Lady Mary's memory. "I am glad it was so," she said to herself when she was alone, with youthful extravagance. "I am glad it was so; for now no one can think that I loved her for anything but herself."

The household, however, was agitated by all these rumors and inventions. Alice, Connie's elder sister, declined to sleep any longer in that which began to be called the haunted room. She, too, began to think she saw something, she could not tell what, gliding out of the room as it began to get dark, and to hear sighs and moans in the corridors. The servants, who all wanted to leave, and the villagers, who avoided the grounds after nightfall, spread the rumor far and near that the house was haunted.

XI.

In the meantime, Connie herself was silent, and saw no more of the lady. Her attachment to Mary grew into one of those visionary passions which little girls so often form for young women. She followed her so-called governess wherever she went, hanging upon her arm when she could, holding her dress when no other hold was possible,--following her everywhere, like her shadow. The vicarage, jealous and annoyed at first, and all the neighbors indignant too, to see Mary transformed into a dependent of the city family, held out as long as possible against the good-nature of Mrs. Turner, and were revolted by the spectacle of this child claiming poor Mary's attention wherever she moved. But by-and-by all these strong sentiments softened, as was natural. The only real drawback was, that amid all these agitations Mary lost her bloom. She began to droop and grow pale under the observation of the watchful doctor, who had never been otherwise than dissatisfied with the new position of affairs, and betook himself to Mrs. Bowyer for sympathy and information. "Did you ever see a girl so fallen off?" he said. "Fallen off, doctor! I think she is prettier and prettier every day." "Oh," the poor man cried, with a strong breathing of impatience, "You ladies think of nothing, but prettiness!--was I talking of prettiness? She must have lost a stone since she went back there. It is all very well to laugh," the doctor added, growing red with suppressed anger, "but I can tell you that is the true test. That little Connie Turner is as well as possible; she has handed over her nerves to Mary Vivian. I wonder now if she ever talks to you on that subject."

"Who? little Connie?"

"Of course I mean Miss Vivian, Mrs. Bowyer. Don't you know the village is all in a tremble about the ghost at the Great House?"

"Oh yes, I know, and it is very strange. I can't help thinking, doctor,--"

"We had better not discuss that subject. Of course I don't put a moment's faith in any such nonsense. But girls are full of fancies. I want you to find out for me whether she has begun to think she sees anything. She looks like it; and if something isn't done she will soon do so, if not now."

"Then you do think there is something to see," said Mrs. Bowyer, clasping her hands; "that has always been my opinion: what so natural--?"

"As that Lady Mary, the greatest old aristocrat in the world, should come and make private revelations to Betsey Barnes, the under housemaid--?" said the doctor, with a sardonic grin.

"I don't mean that, doctor; but if she could not rest in her grave, poor old lady--"

"You think, then, my dear," said the vicar, "that Lady Mary, an old friend, who was as young in her mind as any of us, lies body and soul in that old dark hole of a vault?"

"How you talk, Francis! what can a woman say between you horrid men? I say if she couldn't rest,--wherever she is,--because of leaving Mary destitute, it would be only natural,--and I should think the more of her for it," Mrs. Bowyer cried.

The vicar had a gentle professional laugh over the confusion of his wife's mind. But the doctor took the matter more seriously. "Lady Mary is safely buried and done with, I am not thinking of her," he said; "but I am thinking of Mary Vivian's senses, which will not stand this much longer. Try and find out from her if she sees anything: if she has come to that, whatever she says we must have her out of there."

But Mrs. Bowyer had nothing to report when this conclave of friends met again. Mary would not allow that she had seen anything. She grew paler every day, her eyes grew larger, but she made no confession; and Connie bloomed and grew, and met no more old ladies upon the stairs.

XII.

The days passed on, and no new event occurred in this little history. It came to be summer,--balmy and green,--and everything around the old house was delightful, and its beautiful rooms became more pleasant than ever in the long days and soft brief nights. Fears of the earl's return and of the possible end of the Turners' tenancy began to disturb the household, but no one so much as Mary, who felt herself to cling as she had never done before to the old house. She had never got over the impression that a secret presence, revealed to no one else, was continually near her, though she saw no one. And her health was greatly affected by this visionary double life.

This was the state of affairs on a certain soft wet day when the family were all within doors. Connie had exhausted all her means of amusement in the morning. When the afternoon came, with its long, dull, uneventful hours, she had nothing better to do than to fling herself upon Miss Vivian, upon whom she had a special claim. She came to Mary's room, disturbing the strange quietude of that place, and amused herself looking over all the trinkets and ornaments that were to be found there, all of which were associated to Mary with her godmother. Connie tried on the bracelets and brooches which Mary in her deep mourning had not worn, and asked a hundred questions. The answer which had to be so often repeated, "That was given to me by my godmother," at last called forth the child's remark, "How fond your godmother must have been of you, Miss Vivian! She seems to have given you everything--"

"Everything!" cried Mary, with a full heart.

"And yet they all say she was not kind enough," said little Connie,--"what do they mean by that? for you seem to love her very much still, though she is dead. Can one go on loving people when they are dead?"

"Oh yes, and better than ever," said Mary; "for often you do not know how you loved them, or what they were to you, till they are gone away."

Connie gave her governess a hug and said, "Why did not she leave you all her money, Miss Vivian? everybody says she was wicked and unkind to die without--"

"My dear," cried Mary, "do not repeat what ignorant people say, because it is not true."

"But mamma said it, Miss Vivian."

"She does not know, Connie,--you must not say it. I will tell your mamma she must not say it; for nobody can know so well as I do,--and it is not true--"

"But they say," cried Connie, "that that is why she can't rest in her grave. You must have heard. Poor old lady, they say she cannot rest in her grave, because--"

Mary seized the child in her arms with a pressure that hurt Connie. "You must not! You must not!" she cried, in a sort of panic. Was she afraid that some one might hear? She gave Connie a hurried kiss, and turned her face away, looking out into the vacant room. "It is not true! it is not true!" she cried, with a great excitement and horror, as if to stay a wound. "She was always good, and like an angel to me. She is with the angels. She is with God. She cannot be disturbed by anything--anything! Oh, let us never say, or think, or imagine--" Mary cried. Her cheeks burned, her eyes were full of tears. It seemed to her that something of wonder and anguish and dismay was in the room round her,--as if some one unseen had heard a bitter reproach, an accusation undeserved, which must wound to the very heart.

Connie struggled a little in that too tight hold. "Are you frightened, Miss Vivian? What are you frightened for? No one can hear; and if you mind it so much, I will never say it again."

"You must never, never say it again. There is nothing I mind so much," Mary said.

"Oh," said Connie, with mild surprise. Then, as Mary's hold relaxed, she put her arms round her beloved companion's neck. "I will tell them all you don't like it. I will tell them they must not--oh!" cried Connie again, in a quick astonished voice. She clutched Mary round the neck, returning the violence of the grasp which had hurt her, and with the other hand pointed to the door. "The lady! the lady! oh, come and see where she is going!" Connie cried.

Mary felt as if the child in her vehemence lifted her from her seat. She had no sense that her own limbs or her own will carried her, in the impetuous rush with which Connie flew. The blood mounted to her head. She felt a heat and throbbing as if her spine were on fire. Connie holding by her skirts, pushing her on, went along the corridor to the other door, now deserted, of Lady Mary's room. "There, there! don't you see her? She is going in!" the child cried, and rushed on, clinging to Mary, dragging her on, her light hair streaming, her little white dress waving.

Lady Mary's room was unoccupied and cold,--cold, though it was summer, with the chill that rests in uninhabited apartments. The blinds were drawn down over the windows; a sort of blank whiteness, greyness, was in the place, which no one ever entered. The child rushed on with eager gestures, crying, "Look! look!" turning her lively head from side to side. Mary, in a still and passive expectation, seeing nothing, looking mechanically to where Connie told her to look, moving like a creature in a dream, against her will, followed. There was nothing to be seen. The blank, the vacancy, went to her heart. She no longer thought of Connie or her vision. She felt the emptiness with a desolation such as she had never felt before. She loosed her arm with something like impatience from the child's close clasp. For months she had not entered the room which was associated with so much of her life. Connie and her cries and warnings passed from her mind like the stir of a bird or a fly. Mary felt herself alone with her dead, alone with her life, with all that had been and that never could be again. Slowly, without knowing what she did, she sank upon her knees. She raised her face in the blank of desolation about her to the unseen heaven. Unseen! unseen! whatever we may do. God above us, and those who have gone from us, and He who has taken them, who has redeemed them, who is ours and theirs, our only hope,--but all unseen, unseen, concealed as much by the blue skies as by the dull blank of that roof. Her heart ached and cried into the unknown. "O God," she cried, "I do not know where she is, but Thou art everywhere. O God, let her know that I have never blamed her, never wished it otherwise, never ceased to love her, and thank her, and bless her. God! God!" cried Mary, with a great and urgent cry, as if it were a man's name. She knelt there for a moment before her senses failed her, her eyes shining as if they would burst from their sockets, her lips dropping apart, her countenance like marble.

XIII.

And *she* was standing there all the time," said Connie, crying and telling her little tale after Mary had been carried away,--"standing with her hand upon that cabinet, looking and looking, oh, as if she wanted to say something and couldn't. Why couldn't she, mamma? Oh, Mr. Bowyer, why couldn't she, if she wanted so much? Why wouldn't God let her speak?"

XIV.

Mary had a long illness, and hovered on the verge of death. She said a great deal in her wanderings about some one who had looked at her. "For a moment, a moment," she would cry; "only a moment! and I had so much to say." But as she got better, nothing was said to her about this face she had seen. And perhaps it was only the suggestion of some feverish dream. She was taken away, and was a long time getting up her strength; and in the meantime the Turners insisted that the chains should be thoroughly seen to, which were not all in a perfect state. And the earl coming to see the place, took a fancy to it, and determined to keep it in his own hands. He was a friendly person, and his ideas of decoration were quite different from those of his grandmother. He gave away a great deal of her old furniture, and sold the rest.

Among the articles given away was the Italian cabinet, which the vicar had always had a fancy for; and naturally it had not been in the vicarage a day, before the boys insisted on finding out the way of opening the secret drawer. And there the paper was found, in the most natural way, without any trouble or mystery at all.

XV.

They all gathered to see the wanderer coming back. She was not as she had been when she went away. Her face, which had been so easy, was worn with trouble; her eyes were deep with things unspeakable. Pity and knowledge were in the lines, which time had not made. It was a great event in that place to see one come back who did not come by the common way. She was received by the great officer who had given her permission to go, and her companions who had received her at the first all came forward, wondering, to hear what she had to say; because it only occurs to those wanderers who have gone back to earth of their own will, to return when they have accomplished what they wished, or it is judged above that there is nothing possible more. Accordingly, the question was on all their lips, "You have set the wrong right,--you have done what you desired?"

"Oh," she said, stretching out her hands, "how well one is in one's own place! how blessed to be at home! I have seen the trouble and sorrow in the earth till my heart is sore, and sometimes I have been near to die."

"But that is impossible," said the man who had loved her.

"If it had not been impossible, I should have died," she said. "I have stood among people who loved me, and they have not seen me nor known me, nor heard my cry. I have been outcast from all life, for I belonged to none. I have longed for you all, and my heart has failed me. Oh how lonely it is in the world, when you are a wanderer, and can be known of none--"

"You were warned," said he who was in authority, "that it was more bitter than death." "What is death?" she said; and no one made any reply. Neither did any one venture to ask her again whether she had been successful in her mission. But at last, when the warmth of her appointed home had melted the ice about her heart, she smiled once more and spoke.

"The little children knew me. They were not afraid of me; they held out their arms. And God's dear and innocent creatures--" She wept a few tears, which were sweet after the ice tears she had shed upon the earth. And then some one, more bold than the rest, asked again, "And did you accomplish what you wished?"

She had come to herself by this time, and the dark lines were melting from her face. "I am forgiven," she said, with a low cry of happiness. "She whom I wronged, loves me and blessed me; and we saw each other face to face. I know nothing more."

"There is no more," said all together. For everything is included in pardon and love.

The Codes Of Hammurabi And Moses
W. W. Davies

QTY

The discovery of the Hammurabi Code is one of the greatest achievements of archaeology, and is of paramount interest, not only to the student of the Bible, but also to all those interested in ancient history...

Religion   ISBN: *1-59462-338-4*   **Pages:132**
MSRP $12.95

The Theory of Moral Sentiments
Adam Smith

QTY

This work from 1749. contains original theories of conscience amd moral judgment and it is the foundation for systemof morals.

Philosophy ISBN: *1-59462-777-0*   **Pages:536**
MSRP $19.95

Jessica's First Prayer
Hesba Stretton

QTY

In a screened and secluded corner of one of the many railway-bridges which span the streets of London there could be seen a few years ago, from five o'clock every morning until half past eight, a tidily set-out coffee-stall, consisting of a trestle and board, upon which stood two large tin cans, with a small fire of charcoal burning under each so as to keep the coffee boiling during the early hours of the morning when the work-people were thronging into the city on their way to their daily toil...

Pages:84

Childrens   ISBN: *1-59462-373-2*   *MSRP $9.95*

My Life and Work
Henry Ford

QTY

Henry Ford revolutionized the world with his implementation of mass production for the Model T automobile. Gain valuable business insight into his life and work with his own auto-biography... "We have only started on our development of our country we have not as yet, with all our talk of wonderful progress, done more than scratch the surface. The progress has been wonderful enough but..."

Pages:300

Biographies/   ISBN: *1-59462-198-5*   *MSRP $21.95*

The Art of Cross-Examination
Francis Wellman

QTY

I presume it is the experience of every author, after his first book is published upon an important subject, to be almost overwhelmed with a wealth of ideas and illustrations which could readily have been included in his book, and which to his own mind, at least, seem to make a second edition inevitable. Such certainly was the case with me; and when the first edition had reached its sixth impression in five months, I rejoiced to learn that it seemed to my publishers that the book had met with a sufficiently favorable reception to justify a second and considerably enlarged edition. ...

Pages:412

Reference   **ISBN:** *1-59462-647-2*   *MSRP $19.95*

On the Duty of Civil Disobedience
Henry David Thoreau

QTY

Thoreau wrote his famous essay, On the Duty of Civil Disobedience, as a protest against an unjust but popular war and the immoral but popular institution of slave-owning. He did more than write—he declined to pay his taxes, and was hauled off to gaol in consequence. Who can say how much this refusal of his hastened the end of the war and of slavery ?

Law   **ISBN:** *1-59462-747-9*   **Pages:48**

MSRP $7.45

Dream Psychology Psychoanalysis for Beginners
Sigmund Freud

QTY

Sigmund Freud, born Sigismund Schlomo Freud (May 6, 1856 - September 23, 1939), was a Jewish-Austrian neurologist and psychiatrist who co-founded the psychoanalytic school of psychology. Freud is best known for his theories of the unconscious mind, especially involving the mechanism of repression; his redefinition of sexual desire as mobile and directed towards a wide variety of objects; and his therapeutic techniques, especially his understanding of transference in the therapeutic relationship and the presumed value of dreams as sources of insight into unconscious desires.

Pages:196

Psychology   **ISBN:** *1-59462-905-6*   *MSRP $15.45*

The Miracle of Right Thought
Orison Swett Marden

QTY

Believe with all of your heart that you will do what you were made to do. When the mind has once formed the habit of holding cheerful, happy, prosperous pictures, it will not be easy to form the opposite habit. It does not matter how improbable or how far away this realization may see, or how dark the prospects may be, if we visualize them as best we can, as vividly as possible, hold tenaciously to them and vigorously struggle to attain them, they will gradually become actualized, realized in the life. But a desire, a longing without endeavor, a yearning abandoned or held indifferently will vanish without realization.

Pages:360

Self Help   **ISBN:** *1-59462-644-8*   *MSRP $25.45*

www.**bookjungle**.com *email: sales@bookjungle.com fax: 630-214-0564 mail: Book Jungle PO Box 2226 Champaign, IL 61825*

QTY

The Rosicrucian Cosmo-Conception Mystic Christianity *by Max Heindel*   ISBN: *1-59462-188-8*   **$38.95**
The Rosicrucian Cosmo-conception is not dogmatic, neither does it appeal to any other authority than the reason of the student. It is: not controversial, but is: sent forth in the, hope that it may help to clear...   New Age/Religion Pages 646

Abandonment To Divine Providence *by Jean-Pierre de Caussade*   ISBN: *1-59462-228-0*   **$25.95**
"The Rev. Jean Pierre de Caussade was one of the most remarkable spiritual writers of the Society of Jesus in France in the 18th Century. His death took place at Toulouse in 1751. His works have gone through many editions and have been republished...   Inspirational/Religion Pages 400

Mental Chemistry *by Charles Haanel*   ISBN: *1-59462-192-6*   **$23.95**
Mental Chemistry allows the change of material conditions by combining and appropriately utilizing the power of the mind. Much like applied chemistry creates something new and unique out of careful combinations of chemicals the mastery of mental chemistry...   New Age Pages 354

The Letters of Robert Browning and Elizabeth Barret Barrett 1845-1846 vol II   ISBN: *1-59462-193-4*   **$35.95**
by Robert Browning and Elizabeth Barrett   Biographies Pages 596

Gleanings In Genesis (volume I) *by Arthur W. Pink*   ISBN: *1-59462-130-6*   **$27.45**
Appropriately has Genesis been termed "the seed plot of the Bible" for in it we have, in germ form, almost all of the great doctrines which are afterwards fully developed in the books of Scripture which follow...   Religion/Inspirational Pages 420

The Master Key *by L. W. de Laurence*   ISBN: *1-59462-001-6*   **$30.95**
In no branch of human knowledge has there been a more lively increase of the spirit of research during the past few years than in the study of Psychology, Concentration and Mental Discipline. The requests for authentic lessons in Thought Control, Mental Discipline and...   New Age/Business Pages 422

The Lesser Key Of Solomon Goetia *by L. W. de Laurence*   ISBN: *1-59462-092-X*   **$9.95**
This translation of the first book of the "Lernegton" which is now for the first time made accessible to students of Talismanic Magic was done, after careful collation and edition, from numerous Ancient Manuscripts in Hebrew, Latin, and French...   New Age/Occult Pages 92

Rubaiyat Of Omar Khayyam *by Edward Fitzgerald*   ISBN: *1-59462-332-5*   **$13.95**
Edward Fitzgerald, whom the world has already learned, in spite of his own efforts to remain within the shadow of anonymity, to look upon as one of the rarest poets of the century, was born at Bredfield, in Suffolk, on the 31st of March, 1809. He was the third son of John Purcell...   Music Pages 172

Ancient Law *by Henry Maine*   ISBN: *1-59462-128-4*   **$29.95**
The chief object of the following pages is to indicate some of the earliest ideas of mankind, as they are reflected in Ancient Law, and to point out the relation of those ideas to modern thought.   Religion/History Pages 452

Far-Away Stories *by William J. Locke*   ISBN: *1-59462-129-2*   **$19.45**
"Good wine needs no bush, but a collection of mixed vintages does. And this book is just such a collection. Some of the stories I do not want to remain buried for ever in the museum files of dead magazine-numbers an author's not unpardonable vanity..."   Fiction Pages 272

Life of David Crockett *by David Crockett*   ISBN: *1-59462-250-7*   **$27.45**
"Colonel David Crockett was one of the most remarkable men of the times in which he lived. Born in humble life, but gifted with a strong will, an indomitable courage, and unremitting perseverance...   Biographies/New Age Pages 424

Lip-Reading *by Edward Nitchie*   ISBN: *1-59462-206-X*   **$25.95**
Edward B. Nitchie, founder of the New York School for the Hard of Hearing, now the Nitchie School of Lip-Reading, Inc, wrote "LIP-READING Principles and Practice". The development and perfecting of this meritorious work on lip-reading was an undertaking...   How-to Pages 400

A Handbook of Suggestive Therapeutics, Applied Hypnotism, Psychic Science   ISBN: *1-59462-214-0*   **$24.95**
by Henry Munro   Health/New Age/Health/Self-help Pages 376

A Doll's House: and Two Other Plays *by Henrik Ibsen*   ISBN: *1-59462-112-8*   **$19.95**
Henrik Ibsen created this classic when in revolutionary 1848 Rome. Introducing some striking concepts in playwriting for the realist genre, this play has been studied the world over.   Fiction/Classics/Plays 308

The Light of Asia *by sir Edwin Arnold*   ISBN: *1-59462-204-3*   **$13.95**
In this poetic masterpiece, Edwin Arnold describes the life and teachings of Buddha. The man who was to become known as Buddha to the world was born as Prince Gautama of India but he rejected the worldly riches and abandoned the reigns of power when...   Religion/History/Biographies Pages 170

The Complete Works of Guy de Maupassant *by Guy de Maupassant*   ISBN: *1-59462-157-8*   **$16.95**
"For days and days, nights and nights, I had dreamed of that first kiss which was to consecrate our engagement, and I knew not on what spot I should put my lips..."   Fiction/Classics Pages 240

The Art of Cross-Examination *by Francis L. Wellman*   ISBN: *1-59462-309-0*   **$26.95**
Written by a renowned trial lawyer, Wellman imparts his experience and uses case studies to explain how to use psychology to extract desired information through questioning.   How-to/Science/Reference Pages 408

Answered or Unanswered? *by Louisa Vaughan*   ISBN: *1-59462-248-5*   **$10.95**
Miracles of Faith in China   Religion Pages 112

The Edinburgh Lectures on Mental Science (1909) *by Thomas*   ISBN: *1-59462-008-3*   **$11.95**
This book contains the substance of a course of lectures recently given by the writer in the Queen Street Hall, Edinburgh. Its purpose is to indicate the Natural Principles governing the relation between Mental Action and Material Conditions...   New Age/Psychology Pages 148

Ayesha *by H. Rider Haggard*   ISBN: *1-59462-301-5*   **$24.95**
Verily and indeed it is the unexpected that happens! Probably if there was one person upon the earth from whom the Editor of this, and of a certain previous history, did not expect to hear again...   Classics Pages 380

Ayala's Angel *by Anthony Trollope*   ISBN: *1-59462-352-X*   **$29.95**
The two girls were both pretty, but Lucy who was twenty-one who supposed to be simple and comparatively unattractive, whereas Ayala was credited, as her Bombwhat romantic name might show, with poetic charm and a taste for romance. Ayala when her father died was nineteen...   Fiction Pages 484

The American Commonwealth *by James Bryce*   ISBN: *1-59462-286-8*   **$34.45**
An interpretation of American democratic political theory. It examines political mechanics and society from the perspective of Scotsman James Bryce   Politics Pages 572

Stories of the Pilgrims *by Margaret P. Pumphrey*   ISBN: *1-59462-116-0*   **$17.95**
This book explores pilgrims religious oppression in England as well as their escape to Holland and eventual crossing to America on the Mayflower, and their early days in New England...   History Pages 268

QTY

The Fasting Cure *by Sinclair Upton*   ISBN: *1-59462-222-1*   **$13.95**

In the Cosmopolitan Magazine for May, 1910, and in the Contemporary Review (London) for April, 1910, I published an article dealing with my experiences in fasting. I have written a great many magazine articles, but never one which attracted so much attention... New Age/Self Help/Health Pages 164

Hebrew Astrology *by Sepharial*   ISBN: *1-59462-308-2*   **$13.45**

In these days of advanced thinking it is a matter of common observation that we have left many of the old landmarks behind and that we are now pressing forward to greater heights and to a wider horizon than that which represented the mind-content of our progenitors...   Astrology Pages 144

Thought Vibration or The Law of Attraction in the Thought World   ISBN: *1-59462-127-6*   **$12.95**

by William Walker Atkinson   *Psychology/Religion Pages 144*

Optimism *by Helen Keller*   ISBN: *1-59462-108-X*   **$15.95**

Helen Keller was blind, deaf, and mute since 19 months old, yet famously learned how to overcome these handicaps, communicate with the world, and spread her lectures promoting optimism. An inspiring read for everyone...   Biographies/Inspirational Pages 84

Sara Crewe *by Frances Burnett*   ISBN: *1-59462-360-0*   **$9.45**

In the first place, Miss Minchin lived in London. Her home was a large, dull, tall one, in a large, dull square, where all the houses were alike, and all the sparrows were alike, and where all the door-knockers made the same heavy sound...   Childrens/Classic Pages 88

The Autobiography of Benjamin Franklin *by Benjamin Franklin*   ISBN: *1-59462-135-7*   **$24.95**

The Autobiography of Benjamin Franklin has probably been more extensively read than any other American historical work, and no other book of its kind has had such ups and downs of fortune. Franklin lived for many years in England, where he was agent...   Biographies/History Pages 332

Name	
Email	
Telephone	
Address	
City, State ZIP	

☐ **Credit Card**   ☐ **Check / Money Order**

Credit Card Number	
Expiration Date	
Signature	

Please Mail to: Book Jungle
PO Box 2226
Champaign, IL 61825
or Fax to: 630-214-0564

ORDERING INFORMATION

web*: www.bookjungle.com*
email*: sales@bookjungle.com*
fax*: 630-214-0564*
mail*: Book Jungle PO Box 2226 Champaign, IL 61825*
or PayPal *to sales@bookjungle.com*

Please contact us for bulk discounts

DIRECT-ORDER TERMS

20% Discount if You Order
Two or More Books
Free Domestic Shipping!
Accepted: Master Card, Visa,
Discover, American Express

www.ingramcontent.com/pod-product-compliance
Lightning Source LLC
Chambersburg PA
CBHW081159170626
46813CB00009B/3250